"You're pregnant?"

Seth asked.

"Yes," Mariah replied. "With your child, Seth. I guess our one night together was a little more 'productive' than we thought."

"I'd say so." Seth hadn't meant to sound sarcastic. But this woman had haunted his dreams since they'd first met two months ago. Now she was back, and all he wanted to do was pick her up in his arms and hold her until…forever.

"I didn't come back to tell you this and make you feel guilty. But I wa ... d to know both of his or he ... hose parents d ... well thems ...

Seth ju ... eautiful features ... exy smile, at those lips that r ... wild, and he knew their child woul ... be perfect.

And he also knew he didn't want to miss a single moment of it….

Dear Reader,

How does a family get started?

I know what you're thinking, but before that, doesn't it start with the real human need to care and be cared for?

You hold in your hands one of my most emotionally gripping stories. In it you will meet two of the loneliest, neediest characters imaginable. Seth and Mariah are both at loose ends when they discover each other one fateful night, and they are drawn together by the simple need to connect with someone. That connection is a beginning, but it isn't enough. They are both so headstrong and so heart-tender that they have isolated themselves, each in a different way, for protection. But now the connection has been made, and there are new needs that must be met.

How can two people who are powerfully attracted but hardly know each other become the nucleus of a new family? Where are the seeds of trust for two people whom the world has badly used? High in the mountain wilderness of Montana Seth and Mariah meet again, and there they start over. The attraction has been undeniable from the beginning, but the caring has yet to be discovered. In the fertile bed of caring, a family takes root.

It all begins with two people who need to be together....

Kathleen Eagle

KATHLEEN EAGLE

'Til There Was You

Silhouette Books

Published by Silhouette Books

America's Publisher of Contemporary Romance

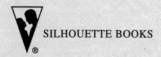

SILHOUETTE BOOKS

ISBN-13: 978-0-373-36144-1
ISBN-10:   0-373-36144-0

'TIL THERE WAS YOU

Copyright © 1990 by Kathleen Eagle

Visit Silhouette Books at www.eHarlequin.com

Printed in U.S.A.

KATHLEEN EAGLE

After more than forty books, including several *New York Times* and *USA TODAY* bestsellers, this award-winning author continues to mine the mysteries of the human heart in ways that touch readers around the world. A transplanted New Englander, Kathleen is the author of the first romance novel to be a finalist for the prestigious Minnesota Book Award. She is a former teacher on the Standing Rock Reservation of the Lakota Nation and still teaches at the Loft Literary Center in Minneapolis, Minnesota.

For my brother, Dan, who served his country in proud Pierson tradition, and for Donna, his wife.

Chapter One

Seth Cantrell liked the way his farcical falsetto sent the few remembered snatches of an old tune skipping like thin, flat stones over the treetops below him. "The mountain hi-i-ee-i-ee-igh—" His voice dropped, a heavy chunk of granite this time tumbling down "the val-ley be-low-ho-ho." It was a human voice, even if it was only his own, and the sound helped him keep things in perspective. He wasn't a bear, a wolf or a ram. He kept company with those creatures, but man was surely the only animal whose call of the wild was off-key rock and roll. In this western Montana wilderness, Seth's howl was in a class by itself.

Daylight was dropping behind the blue-gray peaks, casting ripples of lavender into the puffy bellies of cirrus clouds. The log and stone cabin, tucked against an escarpment and flanked by fir saplings, was a welcome sight. There would be enough water in the holding tank for a shower, and he wanted to soak his feet. He hadn't been able to confirm the reports of poachers on the North Slope, but he'd done a lot of climbing in the attempt. Shale shards crackled under the pressure of his heavy rubber-soled boots—the first damn things he'd kick off the minute he hit the cabin. He would sign over his life savings to the helicopter pilot who could bring him a masseuse right about now, preferably one who was willing to stay the night.

The first sign of trouble was the unbolted cabin door. There wasn't a bear afoot who could manipulate that bolt. Seth unsnapped the flap of his holster and drew out a .44 pistol as he stepped more cautiously. He wasn't an alarmist, not anymore, but lately there had been some strange goings-on in his territory. It struck him first that someone had intruded on his personal space, and only as an afterthought that this was federal property. Worst of all, somebody was in there and had been listening to him sing. Seth Cantrell didn't sing for *anybody*. He held the pistol discreetly next to his thigh as he pushed the heavy wooden door open and peered into the cabin's dark interior.

The light from the open door fell across the plank floor. There was no intruder sitting at the table or on the split-log settee that faced the stone hearth. Seth scanned the room from corner to corner before he spotted the lump of bedding on the cot against the far wall.

Who's been sleeping in my bed? the big bear grumbled.

He stepped across the threshold and closed the door. He set a chair next to the bed, straddled it and draped his gun hand over the chair's low backrest as he reached over to pull back the bedroll.

The face was childlike in its softness. Presumably there

was some kind of hair stuffed under the blue knit ski hat, and beneath the hiker's lightweight sleeping bag there was probably some indication of gender, but in the dusky shadows of the cabin this sleeping face revealed nothing but youth and innocence. Seth glanced at the pistol, then back to the face. The sleeping bag was one of those new-fangled heat-retaining jobs with a lining that resembled aluminum foil. He gripped the corner of it as part of his mind growled, *What the hell...?* The silky silver lining framed the youthful face with an ethereal aura, and he almost felt as though he were the one who was trespassing. He peeled the bedding away and gently shook his visitor's shoulder.

"Hey."

The voice in her ear was rich and warm.

"Are you lost?"

"Mmm." She snuggled deeper into the darkness. "Just tired."

Female. A sweet, feminine voice. Maybe his mind was playing tricks on him. He hadn't seen a woman in, what? A couple of months? But he couldn't see much of one in this bundle, either. "Wake up, now. Tell me who you are and how you got here. You're lost, aren't you?"

Reluctantly she opened her eyes. She saw a dark silhouette, a thatch of black hair, big shoulders. He smelled of pine pitch, and his voice enveloped her like a deep, warm pocket, just as it had that night. She propped herself up on her elbow. Her voice was scratchy with sleep. "I was hiking."

"You're pretty far off the trails. Are you alone?"

She saw the pistol, and she sat up straighter.

He glanced at the weapon in his hand. "I won't hurt you as long as you do me the same favor. Deal?" She nodded quickly, and he holstered the pistol. "Did you get separated from your party or something?"

"No. I'm alone."

She folded her legs like a jackknife and sat upright, emerging from the black shadows into the gray ones. There was something familiar about her eyes. He couldn't discern the color, but there was something about the way they glistened. Seth tried to put that spark together with the scrubbed-clean look. Her nose and cheeks were shiny with some kind of protective grease. In the gray light, her face was nearly colorless.

"That isn't too smart. Hiking alone in this part of the country is pretty damned dangerous."

She felt a sudden, sickening tightness in her chest. He didn't recognize her. He didn't remember her at all. She remembered thinking that his dark eyes had seemed to absorb her thoughts and leave her no secrets. But he didn't even remember.

"Maybe I did get a little off track," she admitted, "but I'm an experienced hiker."

She didn't look like an experienced anything. She couldn't have been more than sixteen.

"I don't suppose you have a permit?" he asked.

He loomed close to her in the dark, the same pine-scented, hulking shadow she remembered discovering on the balcony at Telly's chalet two months ago....

"You're not one of Telly's regulars."

He startled her. Mariah hadn't seen him standing off to the side under the steep pitch of the eave. It was raining, a steady downpour, and she stopped just short of stepping beyond the sheltering overhang and getting soaked. Cool rain would have felt good, because she was dance-party hot. But she turned toward the voice.

It was the ranger, the one Telly had made a fuss over when he first came in. He was worth making a fuss over, as imposing a presence as he was, but a quiet fuss. Telly had welcomed him with the comment that he was "too cute to be a mountain hermit," and he told her that he'd heard that, and he'd decided to come down off his mountain to see if it was true. But the look Telly had gotten from him had invited no rejoinder. He'd taken a seat between two men at the bar and ordered a drink.

The summer parties at Telly's Ski Resort drew a collection of locals from Whitefish and even as far as Kalispell, as well as summer-bored ski bums and vacationers. Telly was a people collector. What amused her was the infinite variety of combinations that were possible. Her eyes had flashed, and she had whispered to Mariah that the "tall, dark ranger" was a delicious mystery. Once in a while he showed up for a party, but he kept to himself, much to her disappointment. He was a watcher.

He was watching there on the balcony, and Mariah felt a little uncomfortable, having loosened up at the party downstairs with a couple of tangy margaritas before dancing herself into a sweat. Her skin felt clammy in the cool air. The hard-driving music thudded beneath her. "This is the first time I've been here in the summer," she said as she lifted her hair off the back of her neck. "I like the spring skiing here."

"Where are you from?"

She stood in the window light, while he stayed in the shadows. She took a step closer, but one was all she dared. "Bozeman. You?"

"High country."

"Bozeman is pretty high."

His chuckle was a soft, deep rumble in the dark. "Compared to what?"

She laughed—light laughter—as light as her head. "Compared to Billings or Miles City." Another small step took her out of the pool of light and into his shadows. But she felt light. Light and just a little foolish. *One baby step. Father, may I? Yes, you may.* "How high is this high country of yours?"

From his corner, ice clinked against the sides of a glass. "High enough to take your breath away."

"Telly says you're a ranger." She could see him better now. He gave a brief nod and a grunt that passed for agreement as he drained his glass of all but the ice, then set it aside on a small round table. "Are you with the Forest Service?"

"Not right now." He stepped close to her and put his hands on her shoulders, which were bare. He was so close and so big, he blocked out everything else—the water dripping off the eaves, the cool air, the light from inside. She didn't know where her next breath was coming from. "Right now I'm with you. You like to dance." The fast music faded out, and a slow tempo faded in. He slipped his arm around her. "You like to lose yourself in the music," he added quietly as he moved her, shuffling an inch at a time across the decking.

His hand warmed her bare back, and she was keenly aware of what little she wore—a backless halter dress and a pair of silk panties. More daring than she'd dreamed she could be. She rested her hand on his shoulder for a moment. Leverage. With an unexpected push she could send him back to his corner. She lifted her chin and breathed deeply of the pine scent, then slid her arm around his neck. Never mind the leverage.

"You were watching me down there," she said.

"Me and all the rest of the backwoods boys."

"I do love to dance. I get so few chances."

"Really?" He slid his hand a little higher, his fingers accounting for each vertebra. "What's the matter with the boys in Bozeman?"

"I don't...spend a lot of time in Bozeman."

He chuckled again. "I don't blame you."

"It isn't that." She looked up and found him smiling at her. His brown eyes had trapped pieces of light from the window, and they seemed warm and caring. Somehow *I don't blame you* meant he knew how she felt about everything. "What's your name?"

"Seth."

It was a soft sound, as soft as his lips. He lifted her other hand, laid it on his shoulder and kissed her as he led her in the dance. They made slow circles on the balcony. Cool damp air swept over her back. His hands, moving in slow, caressing circles, chased the chill away. Together they made warm, wet kisses. His tongue traced the roundness of her mouth. She tipped her head to one side to allow him to explore beneath the curve of her jaw. His mouth, his breath, the tip of his tickling tongue, made her shiver, but his hands kept her warm. He nibbled her shoulder, slipped his hands over her hips and held her while he rolled his belly against hers. She tangled her fingers in the thick hair at the back of his neck.

"You're some dancer, Seth." Foolish talk. Light and giddy, like her head. She was a music box dancer, swirling in slow motion.

"You're some partner."

"I know." She tipped her head back and drew a deep breath. "Light on my feet."

He moved his hands slowly up her sides, and his thumbs discovered the wonder of a low-backed halter dress. They crept up to the undersides of her breasts like spies seeking cover, and there they lingered. She should move them, she thought. His touch made her feel reckless, and she knew she should move his hands to a safer place and decline whatever offer he was making.

But she didn't. She banished all sensible thoughts and sought his kiss again. The delicate swirling in her head tightened into a coil and plummeted to her belly, a tiny cyclone, with its devastating point boring deep, deep inside her. She pressed against him where she ached. His thumbs received the signal and moved toward her nipples, in for the kill, circling, teasing, drawing out their prey. Soft flesh tightened, and, oh! sweet misery.

"There's a place close by," he whispered.

"A place?"

"Privacy."

"Oh." It was time to say no, a voice told her. She always listened to that voice. Always. Now was the time.

His thumbs rocked gently. "I want to kiss you here," he said. "And we need a private place."

He moved her through the sliding door into the hallway, giving her the refuge of his arm and the support of his side. It was happening quickly. The seconds, all fat and full of sensations, seemed to tumble over one another. Mariah's head was still back on the balcony, but her body was all atingle, and she was putting one foot in front of the other. She was about to take a giant step without saying, *Father, may I?* But this was *her* step. Seth opened the door and ushered her into a dark office. He was going to kiss her there, where his touch had filled her with the hard need to be kissed.

In an electrical outlet near the floor, a surge-protecting device glowed like a beacon, casting a dim yellow aura. "Telly's sanctuary," Seth said as he closed the door, pushed the knob and gave it a twist. "No one will bother us here."

She wasn't interested in knowing why or how he knew. Not then. She turned to him, and he took her head in his hands, slid his fingers into her hair and studied her face for a moment. Even in near darkness, the intensity in his eyes was visible, almost tangible. She thought he had something to say to her, something stirring, and she was ready to be stirred, wanted to be, waited to be. But no words came. Instead she watched the slow descent of his lips until they were too close, and she had to close her eyes and raise her chin to be stirred by his kiss. He relished her mouth as though it were glazed with frosting that might satisfy his craving for something sweet.

She hardly knew what she craved, but the more he kissed and caressed her, the more immediate her response was. Party music thudded beneath her feet, and her heart pounded with it. She felt her skirt go slack as he slid the zipper from the small of her back, down, down—how deliciously bold! He untied the halter at the back of her neck and gave the dress a nudge at her hips. It slipped to the floor. The sound he made was startling, almost as though she'd wounded him somehow. Stunned, she crossed her arms over her breasts. He started to pull her protection away, but then he stopped and took her in his arms.

"Cold?"

She nodded under his chin.

"You want to call this off?"

"No." Her answer was desperately quick.

"Neither do I. You're beautiful."

"Usually I don't...dress so..."

"I like it," he whispered as he nuzzled her temple. His

hands played over the ins and outs of her French-cut panties. "Makes it easier to kiss you in private places."

Before she could have another negative thought, he covered her mouth with his kiss, and they knelt together in the center of a plush sheepskin throw rug. She lay back, waiting, watching him shed his western shirt, boots and jeans as though he were in his own bedroom. Should a woman tell a man how beautiful he was? In the dark she saw the T-shaped shadow of hair that crossed his broad chest and trailed down to his belly.

He laid his hand between her breasts, and she thought, They're too small. They've flattened out. He won't even be able to find them now. He smiled wistfully, as though he'd read her mind, and slid his hand slowly toward her belly. He leaned down to kiss her, and then he made good his intention to kiss more private places, treating first one breast, then the other, to the delicious attentions of his lips and tongue, setting her whole body ablaze. He caressed her belly, rubbing the silk over her skin, slipping his hand lower, lower, making her moist, making her moan.

He braced himself on his elbow, and his chest hair tickled her hard nipples as he leaned over her. "Touch me," he said, his voice gravelly. "Tell me if I have what you need."

Brightness glistened in a bead of perspiration that slid along his temple. She pressed herself into his palm and welcomed his finger's tentative invasion—oh, sweet contradiction in terms! She reached for him, found him, no, not wanting—found him needing a place inside her. She whispered his name.

"Are you...prepared for this?" he asked.

He wreaked such havoc with the intimate touch of just a finger, and she raised, she reached, she readied, yes!

She would die for this. She held his hard-muscled hips in her hands and lifted herself up to him. The homing was perfect, the sensation sublime.

After the loving, there was still more. He held her, touched her, kissed the curves and hollows of her face. The rain rattled against the windowpane. Little was said, but there was little to say. There was no explanation for it, and God forbid there should have been any apologies. He broke the silence finally by asking her name, and she gave as much as he had given her.

"Mariah."

"No, I don't have a permit," she confessed quietly.

"They wouldn't have given you one to hike alone in grizzly country. But then, an experienced hiker like you knows all that."

"Yes."

She spoke so softly that he had to strain to hear her, yet there was a familiarity that nibbled at his ear. "You're really trespassing, you know. That's my bed."

She glanced down, then up again. "I'm sorry. I've been out for three days, doing a lot of bushwhacking off the beaten path. I thought maybe the station was un-manned, and when I came in, well—" She shrugged in-nocently. "The bed looked so good."

"That's what Goldilocks said." He almost smiled. "Her bears were a little more civilized than the ones we've got up here, though. Where are you from?"

"I—" It hit her again. He really didn't recognize her. She felt as though someone had piled bricks on her chest. "I'm staying at Telly's Ski Resort."

He stared at her, his eyes unreadable. After a moment, he stood up and set the chair aside. He dug into the breast pocket of his flannel shirt and came up with a book of matches. As he touched a flame to the wick of a Coleman lantern, he thought of those eyes. Yes, he knew them. He remembered the way they had flashed when she'd tossed her head and swayed to the music. When he turned to look at her again, her cap was gone. The wealth of auburn hair was shapeless and full of static electricity. Her jacket was zipped up to her neck, and the blush in her cheeks was missing. She'd looked slick and sophisticated the night they'd met. Her dress had been a knockout, baring her long, sleek back. He sure as hell hoped she was older than she appeared to be right now.

She dropped her legs over the side of the bed, and they watched each other. She saw that he recognized her, and she held her breath, hoping for some sign of welcome. Just a smile would do. He saw that she had tucked herself into her fancy bedroll without taking her hiking boots off.

"You look different," he said finally. "I didn't know you."

She thought about the remark for a moment and decided it was true enough, even though it wasn't what she wanted to hear. The lantern cast a yellowish glow, a warning. She felt wary.

"Mariah, right?"

"Yes." Her eyes followed his every move as he opened the metal door of the fireplace, squatted on his heels and began laying a fire.

"It's late September, Mariah. Shouldn't you be back in school?"

She missed the humor because of the question's remarkable insight. She hadn't told him anything about herself. "I...I'm on a leave of absence this year."

He turned and rested one knee on the stone hearth as

he looked back at her. "You're a teacher, then. That's a relief."

"Why?"

"Because it means you're not as young as you look, unless this state's gotten desperate for teachers. What do you teach?"

"Primary grades."

He turned back to his work. "So you're taking the time off to travel the back roads?"

"I ski. Competitively." She weighed each word, trying to decide how many she should parcel out at this point. She wasn't sure she wanted to tell him anything more, but she handed him another bit of information, then another. "So I'm taking a year off to, um, to really give it a shot. That's why I hike. It's part of my training."

He remembered what incredible legs she had. Long, lean and strong. She'd locked them around his waist and made him—"Do you have a map of the area?"

"Yes."

The kindling caught, and flames sprang up like a bright yellow picket fence around the pine logs. He brushed his hands on his jeans as he rose and turned to her. "Did you know this was my station?"

Had there been some hint of welcome, she would have been honest, but his eyes suggested nothing of the way he felt about seeing her now. She glanced away as she told him, "I knew you were a ranger. I guess I should have thought—but I did recognize you right away, and I knew I was in for…some embarrassment. For a minute, I thought maybe you'd…" She couldn't manage the word casually.

"I'd had a lot to drink that night, and so had you." His slow smile came in response to a sensual memory, and he shook his head. "But, no, I haven't forgotten."

Mariah felt as though she had just undressed in front of a stranger. Good Lord, what had she expected? She'd done something crazy that night. People just didn't do things like that, not people like her. But then, that night she'd been different. She'd even dressed differently, and she'd felt different. Liberated, at least temporarily. Free to respond. Free to be sensual. Sexual. Afterward, when they just held each other as though they had all the time in the world, it hadn't seemed to matter how much or how little had gone before. She had something new in her life, and it felt wonderful. Maybe he hadn't come back the next day. Maybe he had his reasons, just as she'd had hers for telling him as little as she did. What they'd shared had been quick and hot, but it had also been unique, and theirs alone. But that was not the way he was looking at her now.

"It was a pretty unusual…" She stood up and made a vain attempt to finger-comb her hair. It crackled and wound itself around her hands like Medusa's snakes. "A strangers-in-the-night sort of thing," she suggested, hoping she sounded unaffected. "I'm sure you didn't expect to run into me again."

"Not here, anyway." The look he gave her suggested he hadn't decided what to make of their encounter yet. "But then, you were a surprise right from the start." He gave a short laugh and headed for the storage room at the back of the cabin. "I'm so hungry I could eat my own cooking," he called out from behind the door. "How about you?"

"I guess so." She felt a little numb. She had envisioned a different kind of reunion. Not long-lost lovers, certainly, but something a little warmer than this. "I didn't expect to run into you, either." It was a protective lie, but a lie nonetheless. "It's certainly awkward."

"Hash and eggs okay?" He appeared in the doorway and punctuated his question with the toss of a can. It smacked back into his palm.

"Fine. I'm not a big eater."

"What have you been living on lately? Trail mix?"

"Just since I've been up here. And huckleberries, of course, and—"

"They're really good this year, aren't they? Ol' Griz is getting fat and sassy."

"Are there many around?"

"Sure." He plunked a skillet down on the burner of a small gas stove, turned on the fuel and struck a match to it. "Haven't you seen any?"

"Not up close."

"Best we keep it that way, for their sake as well as yours. I can take you back down to safer territory in the morning."

She watched him whip up the meal in a matter of minutes. When she offered to set the table, he chuckled at the thought of such a homey chore being performed in his cabin. Sharing supper seemed homey, too, but he knew it would sound silly to a woman like her if he mentioned it. In her long, slender hands, camp plates and utensils looked like the good stuff. She was a skier who could work when she felt like it, or take a year off when she had a yen to play. She'd probably just been slumming when she partied at Telly's, and he'd been a handy nightcap.

Now, suddenly, there she was, as unlikely a guest as she had been at Telly's. And the coincidence was barely credible. He didn't understand why she would want to complicate matters by trekking up the side of his mountain. Only the hardiest and most dedicated hikers ventured this deep into Montana's Flathead River wilderness.

It seemed unlikely that she'd gotten off the track, but somehow he had the feeling that if he asked more questions, he would get answers that might complicate his own life. He didn't want that.

Eating appeared to be a tiresome obligation for her. She chewed each small bite more thoroughly than any fried egg could possibly require while she pushed the food on her plate with her fork as though rearranging it might improve the taste. They spoke of nothing but passing the pepper, and it finally occurred to Seth that Mariah was not bored with the food but uneasy in his company. She sat across from him with that blue windbreaker still zipped up to her chin, her face devoid of makeup except for the greasy remnants of sunscreen. Each time she tried to push that wealth of auburn hair back from her face, it became a pouf of live wire.

She felt his scrutiny, and she glanced up from her plate. He was struck by the look in her eyes. He'd seen it before, and it had affected him then. Clear green eyes. Even when they'd been enhanced with shadows and shading, he'd seen no artifice in them. They'd banished his first postpassion thought of putting his pants on and bidding her a breezy goodbye. Instead, he'd held her in his arms and listened to the rain.

"You can have the bed," he said quietly. "I'll sleep in the observation tower."

She looked relieved. "Do you have a bed up there?"

"I'll make one."

She nodded and plodded through another bite.

"Is it that bad?" She glanced up with a quizzical look. "The food," he clarified. "You act like you're chasing a live snail around on that plate."

"I'm sorry. No, the eggs are fine." Her smile seemed thin. "I guess my stomach's gotten used to trail mix and huckleberries.'' After a moment she added, ''And I guess I'm feeling a little awkward about…putting you to so much trouble.''

His dream of a warm shower had already dissipated. The holding tank wasn't big enough for two. ''I can't offer you all the conveniences, but there's a shower in the back room.''

That brought the sparkle back into her eyes. ''A shower would be wonderful.''

She helped him clean up the table before he ushered her into the storage room. He lit another lantern, hung it on a peg and handed her a towel. ''My laundry service comes about once a month. I get towels and bedding when the chopper brings supplies, so this one's been used a little.'' He shrugged. ''But at least it's dry.''

''Thank you.''

God, her voice was soft. He forced his attention to the little wooden stall in the corner and pointed to the shower head and its chain. ''You have to keep pulling the chain as long as you want water. You shouldn't just keep it running, or you'll run out.''

She nodded, clutching the towel to the front of her windbreaker. There was a wooden drain with planks spaced an inch apart on the floor beneath the shower head. There was no curtain. Soap and shampoo stood on the nearby shelf.

''May I borrow those?'' she asked, pointing to the shelf.

''Help yourself.''

''You'll be up in the tower?''

He nodded. ''Yeah…if you need anything. I'll put some more wood in the firebox. It'll burn all night if you keep the door closed.''

She nodded.

He eyed the towel—*his* towel—clutched in her hands.

She glanced up at his soap, rounded and dished with wear.

They remembered lying naked in each other's arms.

"Okay, well…" He turned abruptly toward the door. "I'll check back with you before I turn in—see if you're all squared away."

"Thank you."

He was babbling like an idiot, he told himself as he stretched his stride for the front door. *See if you're all squared away.* What the hell was that supposed to mean? What had happened that night at Telly's had just *happened.* If it happened again—if it happened up here on home ground, where nobody could make a clean exit— well, if it happened a second time, things were bound to get complicated. He wasn't going to come back to see if she was "all squared away." He didn't want to know what she was wearing to bed, and he didn't want to smell his shampoo in her hair. He repeated the word to himself—*complications.*

Mariah sat by the fireplace and dried her hair. She listened for his footsteps, but the only sound she heard outside the cabin was distant canine howling—first a single voice, then a chorus. Should she bolt the door from the inside or leave it open? Go to bed or wait up? Leave the lamp burning or blow it out? Oh, God, why had she come? This whole thing had been a mistake right from the start.

Bone weary, she crawled into bed, but sleep was a long time coming. She kept listening for those footsteps.

Chapter Two

The lookout tower was the equivalent of four stories tall. Seth knew the minute Mariah placed her foot on the first metal step. At a time when his life had depended on it, he had developed a sixth sense about the proximity of another human being. Within moments he could actually hear her distant footfalls and feel her narrowing the gap. He was surrounded by glass, through which he could view the clear mountain morning, the blue-green timber below and the distant peaks of sedge-covered tundra and rugged gray rock at higher elevations. The tower's only blind spot was directly below it. Seth counted on his sixth sense to fill in for all his blind spots. It worked well—at least in the wild.

He stepped out onto the catwalk to greet her, but she was obviously preoccupied. When she popped through the hole in the decking, she was startled to find him standing there. She bobbled a little, and his hand shot out reflexively to grab her by the elbow. He held on until she climbed safely up to the landing. She looked up, intending to thank him, but she was distracted by a sudden awareness that she was seeing him in the sunlight for the first time. It brightened his eyes, glistened in his dark hair, lent his face an aura of youth even as it deepened the spokes at the corners of his eyes. She saw that he was older than she'd thought—perhaps late thirties—but the sun chased the moody shadows away. Perched on a tower that seemed to buttress the sky, Seth was as beautiful as any creature was in its element. And he knew it, Mariah thought.

"What a view!" She tipped her head to let the wind take her hair away from her face. Now that she'd assessed him thoroughly, he took a step back to give her better access to the mountain view. She turned to him again, smiling this time and squinting against the sun. "It kind of makes you feel—" She rolled her eyes and tilted her head back and forth. "Kind of has the same effect as a margarita."

"It can, until you get used to it. As long as one of us is sober, I think we're all right." When she glanced away, he told himself there was nothing wrong with being upfront about what was between them. The lost waif was a woman again. The sun ignited red sparks in her hair, and the blush in her cheeks was back. What a dolt he'd been yesterday, taking her for a kid. "Come on in and take a look around."

The tower room was four square walls of windows. The frames were painted pale government-issue green, and the few pieces of furniture clearly came from the same source—the white Formica-topped table, the gunmetal gray desk with its vinyl padded chair. Mariah was drawn to the drum-shaped map table in the center of the room. The round map that delineated the area within view of the lookout would be used to pinpoint the location of a fire if one was sighted.

Seth joined her and tapped his finger on a spot on the map. "This," he said as he raised his arm toward the southeast, "is that peak over there. Trumpeter Peak. Over there is Bearded Mountain, and south of that, that jagged one—it's right here on the map—that's just called Point 8541."

"That one should have a name, too."

"What's your last name?" She looked at him, and he raised one eyebrow. "You never told me," he said.

"Crawford."

"Crawford Mountain," he announced, nodding to the south. "It's yours."

"A whole mountain?"

"Sure. I'm a generous man." He spread another map, this one a Forest Service trail guide. "Show me how you got up here."

She glanced down at the map, then gave him an innocent look. "I got lost."

"Were you planning on all the bushwhacking you had to do to get here?"

"N-no. I knew I'd gone wrong somewhere. I'm not sure how I—"

"Well, just show me where you started out and what your plan was, and we'll figure it out. Where did you camp the first night?"

Mariah moved to his side of the table and perused the map. She leaned closer, planted her elbows at the edge of the paper and studied some more. "This isn't the same map I used," she decided. "Is this an update?"

"As a matter of fact, this one's out-of-date. It shows a couple of trails that don't exist. Never have, never will.

I thought maybe this was the map you were using. Then I could have understood how you might have ended up here." He slid the map off the table and replaced it with another one. "Here's the latest one."

It was a copy of the same map she'd used. She knew, of course, that he was right. There were no paths leading up there, and you had to know where you were going to find the blaze marks that Seth himself had probably made. Telly had brought her as close as she could get in her four-wheel drive Jeep and had helped her map out a plan. Telly knew her mountains. She thought the idea was crazy and romantic, and she didn't know why she hadn't thought of it for herself. A night at Seth's station might be worth a little mountain bushwhacking.

"This isn't a place the *experienced hiker* just stumbles on." He waited until Mariah looked up from the map, but when she did, those green eyes admitted nothing. "What are you doing here, Mariah?"

His voice was disarmingly quiet, and she tried to match it, to control her own. "I wasn't looking for you, if that's what you think." Her ears burned when she lied even a little, and she was glad her hair covered them, because she could feel that burning now.

"That's *exactly* what I think. I had no idea I was that good." His smile smacked of cynicism. "You're the first woman who's ever gone to this much trouble to get me back in the sack."

Now her whole face burned, but she managed a clipped retort. "*Back* in the sack? I don't remember that we had any *sack*."

"We've got one now." He jerked his chin toward the sleeping bag he'd left spread out on the floor.

Mariah stared at the army-green bedding and tried hard to remember what had possessed her that night. *Pos-*

sessed was a good word for it. It hadn't mattered who they were or where they were. She'd called it magic. She'd called it magnetism. In the weeks since he'd changed her life, she'd called it a hundred things, but never rashness. Never pure recklessness. Now here she was. What was he supposed to think?

"Is that where you slept last night?"

"Yeah."

"I'm sorry. I've been sleeping on the ground. I could just as easily have slept up here."

It wasn't quite the suggestion he'd expected. He saw that clear-eyed innocence again—the look he hadn't been able to put together with the sexy woman who'd been so ready and willing. He didn't want to deal with any of it, whether it was innocence or guile, not even the apology he probably owed her for the crude things he'd just said. He'd felt a quick, hard, sudden need that night, and he'd dealt with it, but even then she'd made it tough to just leave it at that. And then last night, thinking about her bathing in his shower and sleeping in his bed, he'd lain there listening, shifting from his back to his side and getting stiff all over. Was that where he'd slept? He hadn't slept much.

"Look," he said finally as he took her arm and turned her toward the east windows. "I'm way out of touch with conveniences, so it's no big deal for me to sleep on the floor." He nodded toward the ground. "That cabin was built in the thirties, and the only improvements anyone's made on it since then are the shower, the gas stove and the fireplace insert, which keeps the place warmer than the open hearth. Up here in the tower we've got a battery-powered radio. That and the helicopter are the only contacts I have with the rest of the world, and I like it that way. Every once in a while I take a couple of days, go down to Telly's or sometimes Whitefish, take in the sights, have a few drinks and maybe get lucky.''

The room fell deathly quiet. He'd chosen the words deliberately, but the minute he got them out, he regretted them. He stared hard at the cabin below. "Tact isn't my strong suit," he confessed.

"I've noticed." She moved away, finding the long table to be more deserving of her interest than he was. There were stacks of books and maps, a photograph of a bear here, an elk there, a pile of wildlife magazines. She fingered the spine of a book about grizzlies.

"Would it help if I apologized?"

"For what?" she asked without looking up.

"The things I just said. The, uh…the things that happened between us."

"Are you sorry?"

"I said some pretty rotten things just now. I'm sorry for saying them."

She turned slowly, found him watching her and waited pointedly for the rest.

He shook his head. "I can't be sorry about that night, though."

Why not? she asked silently. Please tell me why not.

"Hell, you were the prettiest thing I'd seen in a long, long time."

Mariah groaned. "If you mean *living* thing, it's hard to take that as a compliment." With a sweeping gesture she indicated the wilderness beyond the surrounding windows. "You've been up here for a long time, looking at a lot of mountain goats."

"Only from a distance." He shoved his hands into the pockets of his jeans and shrugged almost boyishly. "You want me to apologize for not being sorry? Maybe I could manage that."

"Of course I don't." She turned away again, moved to his desk and snatched up a pair of binoculars. She had an urge to *make* him sorry, and she could. She knew she could, but she would hurt herself in the process. Instead, she decided to play the game that seemed to work so well for him.

"I'd always heard Telly's summer parties were a good time. I needed a break, too." She raised the binoculars and tried to find something to look at—a mountain, a tree, anything. Damn, some part of her always seemed to be burning. Now it was her eyes. She blinked furiously and reminded herself that all that burning was what had gotten her into this in the first place. "I guess I got lucky, too."

Seth's back stiffened. That sounded uncomplicated, which was the way he kept telling himself he wanted to keep everything. So why was he staring a hole through her back? Well, at the moment it was better than looking at her face. He sure as hell didn't want her looking him in the eye while she talked about "getting lucky." His words, *his* line, but it sounded different when *she* said it. Maybe it bothered him only because she'd turned his words back on him. Or maybe it was because he was afraid she meant it just the way it sounded.

"It worked out well for both of us, then," he said.

You pigheaded jerk! She swallowed, hoping to soothe that awful pins-and-needles feeling in her throat. "It appears we were both in the right place at the right time that night."

"What about now?" he asked. "Are you...did you find the right place?"

"Certainly not! I got *way* off course yesterday." She slammed the binoculars down on the desk and stared at a distant, jagged peak as though it had offended her.

"Watch it, honey, those belong to the government."

"If they're broken, tell the government to send me a bill—" She was going to do it. She was going to turn away from this window and face him without a trace of disappointment. She took one silent, controlled breath, turned and finished with an icy, *"Honey."*

"I'll help you get back on track, then."

"You already have." They stared at each other through the emotional fog they'd created together. "You gave me a map lesson."

"I'll get my gear together and teach you another lesson." His voice was as devoid of emotion as hers was. "About hiking with a partner."

There was little conversation as they made their descent along narrow mountain ridges. The slopes below them were dappled with bright red and yellow. Only a few patches of summer green still lingered among the deciduous trees. The silent hikers made their way among the tall larches, the spruce and the white pine, and listened to the songs of the Steller's jay and the mountain bluebird. There was no path, but the blaze marks on the trees were familiar to both of them. Seth took the lead, and Mariah followed.

They stopped for a drink from a small creek. He watched her out of the corner of his eye while he scooped up the cold water and drank from his cupped hand. She looked a little winded. She closed her eyes and patted water on her face, then sat back on her heels and contemplated the treetops while she took several slow, deep breaths. He remembered how lean and strong her back had seemed and how muscular her legs were. Dancer's legs, he'd thought at the time. Well, she *had* said she was a skier in training. Maybe she'd been partying all summer and lost her stamina.

"We'll break for lunch," he decided, although ordinarily he would have eaten on the move. "This is a nice spot, huh?"

"It is." She pushed the straps of her backpack off her shoulders and made herself comfortable sitting cross-legged on the brown pine needle carpet. Plastic bags yielded more trail mix—dried fruit, nuts and grain—hardtack and foil packets of soft cheese. A piece of beef jerky appeared under her nose.

"You need some real food, lady."

She looked up and found him smiling, his dark eyes surprisingly sympathetic. She smiled, too, as she accepted the stick of dried meat. "I always manage to eat up all my jerky first."

Leaning close to her, he picked up a plastic pouch half-full of trail mix. "If this is the alternative, I don't blame you." He watched her take a firm hold on the stiff meat and prepare to rip it with her teeth. "So you like jerky, but you're not crazy about hash and eggs."

She had to chew for a moment before she could explain. "I was just tired last night."

"And still dragging a little today?"

"We've done a lot of walking."

"Mostly downhill." He nodded toward the slope below the creek, but something caught his eye, and he scowled.

"What is it?"

He ignored the question as he sprang to his feet and planted only one splattering step in the middle of the creek on his way across. Mariah watched as he examined the claw marks that streaked the bark of a lodgepole pine. He surveyed the ground nearby, then dropped to one knee for a closer look. Dressed in a well-worn fatigue jacket, jeans and butternut Wellington boots, he was unpretentious, self-assured—the protector rather than the hunter. He picked up bits of things from the ground and touched, sniffed, studied, until finally he stood, took one more look around and crossed back again, pausing to swish his hands in the water and wipe them on his jeans.

"We're going back up to the station, and you're gonna have to stay put while I have a look around."

It was Mariah's turn to scowl. "I am?"

"There's a bullet buried in that tree, blood and fur splattered all over hell." He gestured across the creek and added it all up as though he were thinking out loud. "Somebody's poaching bear here. Grizzly, looks like. Can't tell whether they killed him and packed him out. If not, we've got a wounded bear somewhere around. Either way, there's some trigger-happy bastard messing around in my territory, and I don't have time for any more hiking."

"I can find my way down from here."

"I don't doubt that." He raised one thick eyebrow and gave her a pointed look. "But I don't want any lone hikers in my territory, either. Not with poachers and possibly a wounded bear around."

"So what does this mean?"

He bent to retrieve his pack. "Means I'm stuck with you for a couple of days."

"*Stuck* with me?"

"Until the chopper comes." He indicated the assortment of plastic bags lying next to her pack. "Get your stuff together, and let's go."

"What are my other options?" She got to her feet, deliberately moving slowly. She wasn't sure what options she wanted at this point.

He slung his pack over one shoulder, adjusted the straps, then turned to her with a sigh. He still didn't know what she was doing up there, but he was going to have to make peace with the fact that he was probably going to find out. "Look, the chopper'll be here in a couple of days, and I don't have to tell them how long you've been up here, or that you were hiking alone and without a permit—nothing that's going to embarrass you, okay? Unless you might have somebody looking for you, and in that case we can put in a call—"

"No," she answered too quickly. She saw the question in his eyes, and she turned away, knelt and tended to her packing, adding, "I'd rather you wouldn't put in any calls on my account."

He bit off his suggestion that she could hire a private helicopter. He kept telling himself to mind his own business, but she intrigued him more all the time. "You running away from something...or somebody?"

"No." She zipped a pouch without looking up. "I needed some time alone, so I came up here. Sometimes I feel as if there's no time that belongs to me. I thought maybe, for just a little while, if no one knew where I was—" She took the straps of her pack in her hand and paused before she stood up. Their eyes met. "You can understand the need for that kind of time, can't you?"

"Yeah. That much I can understand."

They hiked back up to his sanctuary, and by the time they reached it, she couldn't hide her fatigue. He told her to stay inside the cabin with the door bolted and not to open it for anyone but him. She watched him arm himself with a service revolver and a high-powered shotgun, and he showed her where another rifle was stored away from the view of the rare "trespasser." His final instruction was that she must not leave the cabin while he was gone. She had no thought of it. While he was gone, she slept.

"Mariah! Open up."

Mariah crawled out of Seth's bed, disoriented from the grogginess that took all the satisfaction out of sleeping during the day. It was like a hangover. She yawned and raked her fingers through her hair. "I'm not supposed to let anybody in," she called out.

"It's Seth."

"Seth who?"

"Seth Cantrell. Don't play games."

"You never told me," she muttered as she slid the bolt. "But I knew."

"Knew what?" He smiled. When had a sleepy-eyed woman last greeted him at his door?

She wondered what he could possibly be smiling about. She must have looked like hell. "Your last name. You never bothered to tell me—" she stepped back as he crossed the rustic threshold "—but I bothered to find out."

"You *bothered* to, huh?" He propped the shotgun against the wall and tossed his jacket on the settee. Then he headed for the wood box. "Guess it's time to find out what you're like when you've just gotten up."

"Kind of bearish," she mumbled as she closed the door.

"I like bears."

"Humph." Fix that rumpled bed, she told herself. She hadn't meant to sleep the whole afternoon away.

"'Specially those feisty sows." He hadn't lit a fire before he'd left. Probably should have, he thought as he arranged the kindling. The cabin had grown chilly while she slept. "I know when to keep my distance, though."

"When would that be?"

"After they've been hibernating a while. Somebody wakes 'em up, they're likely to bite his head off just for living."

"Really." The bed was made presentable with a flip of the Indian-print blanket she'd snuggled under. She yawned again and shook her head. "I'm sorry. I'll be better company after I wash my face," she promised as she pointed herself in the direction of the back room.

"I haven't filled the holding tank above the shower, and we haven't gotten any rain, so nothing's running. You'll have to get your water from that big plastic barrel back there. It'll be cold."

"Cold's fine." She hadn't put two and two together the night before. Not only had he given up his bed for her, but also his shower. Showers here were planned in advance. "If you'll give me some ideas, I'll cook supper," she offered.

Ideas. A whoosh of yellow flame engulfed the kindling. He had too damn many ideas, and they'd been driving him crazy the whole time he'd been gone. Unfortunately, food wasn't one of them. "There's a lot of canned stuff in there," he called out as he added pine logs to the fire, one at a time. "See anything that appeals to you?"

He heard the cans sliding around on the shelf. Then came the reality that still surprised him—a feminine voice from the back room. "How about salmon?"

"Sure," he answered. "Salmon's a sure bet for improving any bear's mood."

"I'm a better cook than most bears, but I'm not sure about firing up that stove."

He turned to find that the bear had become a woman again, eyes all asparkle, face dewy and fresh. She held a can in one hand and a cast-iron Dutch oven in the other, and her smile drew him to his feet. "You fill those jeans out better than most bears, too," he said appreciatively.

"There are enough books on bears around here to make you an expert, so I guess you should know."

"I'm an expert on jeans, too." He brushed his hands off on the seat of his own.

"And women?"

"Women? No way. All I know is, some look good in a pair of jeans." He shrugged. "Others don't."

"I wasn't wearing jeans the night we met."

"No, you weren't." He took a match from the box on the mantel and flipped the gas jet on the stove. "You were wearing a dress. I don't know a lot about dresses, but—" The wooden match came to life with a flick of his thumbnail. He held the flame near the burner and watched the fire spread before leveling his gaze at her. "I do remember that one."

"Because of the way I *filled it out*?" she clipped.

A smile pulled at one corner of his mouth, and she saw the memory in his eyes. "Yeah."

It rankled to watch him enjoy that part of the memory. "Strange you didn't ask around about me. At least find out who I was."

"I figured you told me what you wanted me to know."

Which had obviously been enough for him. "Where's the can opener?"

He took one off the shelf above the stove and held his hand out for the can, still assessing her, still remembering. "I imagine when a woman puts on a dress like that, she takes one look at herself in the mirror, and she feels a surge of...energy, maybe?"

"Energy?" She dropped the can into his hand.

"Energy. The kind that made you dance the way you did at the party that night."

"That's the way I always dance." She set the Dutch oven on the stove and took a bowl down from the shelf.

"You danced differently on the balcony." She cast him a sideways glance, and he added, "But the energy was still there. Do you go to a lot of parties? Dance a lot?" The can opener blade bit into the aluminum.

"Actually, no." She remembered having told him that she got few chances. His memory was clearly selective. "In fact, I've only worn that dress once—just that once. It really wasn't my style."

"I'm sure I wasn't your usual style, either." He handed her the can and tossed the ragged lid into the trash.

There was no point in trying to proclaim her innocence. She reminded herself that she wasn't innocent, and she remembered the way she'd tried the new dress on and stood before the mirror, wondering whether the reflection could really be hers. It had looked like somebody she might want to be, at least for the weekend. Somebody who had a life of her own and did things just for fun. "Dynamite," Telly had said. Something explosive. Yes, she'd felt that surge of energy when she looked at herself in the mirror, but it hardly compared with the power she had sensed in him from the moment she'd turned to find him standing there on the balcony. There was nothing lacking in his style. Nothing *usual* about it, either.

Mariah emptied the canned fish into the bowl. "You've got the powdered version of everything I need back there. How about crackers? Do you have any?"

"Sure. What are you making?"

"Salmon loaf," she said as she headed back to the storage room for more ingredients. She returned with powdered eggs, milk, onion and pepper. "I'm going to steam it. How does that sound?"

"Like we might need some water." He handed her a tin of crackers, then unbuckled the holster that was strapped to his waist. "I'll put this away and get you some."

"Did you have any luck?"

He responded with a blank expression.

"Did you find the bear?"

"Only mama bear." She looked offended, and he laughed. "My mistake. It was Goldilocks, or maybe her dark-haired cousin, who was sleeping in my bed. But no real bears."

"You didn't find the hunters, either?"

"Didn't find much of anything, which makes me wonder why the evidence was left behind at the kill site. Whoever it is isn't leaving much of a trail. I think there's a damn good chance there's a wounded bear out there."

Mariah looked up from her mixing. She heard anger in Seth's voice, but there was a kind of confusion in his eyes, almost as though some part of him were trying to outrun the dogged pain of a bullet wound. He wrapped the black leather strap around the holster. "What will you do?" she asked quietly.

"I'll find him," he said distantly. "I'll put him down."

"The bear?"

He looked at her strangely. "Of course."

Cooking was something Mariah knew she did well. Seth seemed surprised, but he praised every aspect of the meal, from the salmon loaf to the compote made from dried fruit. Before they parted company, he would at least like her, Mariah decided. That much had become important to her—that he would come to like her as a person. None of this had turned out the way she'd planned. In those first few moments, when he hadn't recognized her, she'd known it had been a mistake to come. She had ached for him to hold her the way he'd held her that night, but he hadn't even asked her how she'd been.

Watching him eat the meal she had prepared for him, she decided that this would have to be enough. At least she could leave here feeling that they knew each other— that they liked each other. She hadn't decided where she would go when she left, but she had a couple of days to figure that out. She wanted more time than that, but she would take what she could get. She wondered whether her father had reported her missing. Telly was the only one who knew where she was, and Telly would keep her secret.

"You're doing the same thing you did last night." Seth broke into Mariah's reverie and gestured toward her plate with his fork. "So now I know it wasn't my cooking."

"I'm eating," she insisted, and she filled her fork.

"Picking." He pushed his chair back from the table. "Coffee's on me."

"Oh, none for me, thanks."

"What would you like, then? Tea?"

"Just water. This is the best water—"

"Level with me, Mariah." He gripped the edge of the table and told himself he was asking for something he didn't really want, but the first part was out. The way she was acting, he wanted to be prepared. "Are you okay?"

"I'm...fine."

"You sure?" She said she was, didn't she? he asked himself. Just take her word for it.

"Of course." Avoiding his eyes, she reached for his

plate and stacked hers on top of it. "I'm just...maybe it's the altitude or something. I don't have much of an appetite."

That was enough. He didn't want to know any more than that. If she'd just found out that she had some rare disease and was out to indulge all her fantasies before it was too late, he didn't want to know about it.

"I'll get the dishes," he said, and he took them out of her hands. "Tomorrow you'll have water for a shower. For tonight I'll heat enough water so that you can, uh— do whatever you want with it."

She smiled. "What about you?"

"I used one of the lakes this afternoon."

"Brrr." She shivered.

"It builds character."

"Maybe I should try it." He glanced at her over his shoulder, and she shrugged. "Sometimes you just want to try something else, you know? Something that wakes you up and makes you feel really alive."

"A cold mountain lake can sure do that for you." He could think of better ways, but she knew them just as well as he did.

Mariah tried to be helpful, but Seth said she'd done her share. There were no dish towels. He shook the rinse water off the tin plates and stacked them back on the shelves. She brought the salt and pepper from the table and reached to put them back where they belonged, but tiptoes didn't give her quite the height she needed to return them to the spot just above his head. With a soapy, wet hand he took them, shoved them back on the shelf and repeated, "I'll take care of this. Just sit and relax."

He looked almost angry. "Maybe I will have some tea," she said quietly. "Is it in the back room?"

"I'll get it, and I'll make it."

She took a step back.

"What do you want, some kind of a domestic scene?" He pushed the dishpan aside and turned on her, his eyes flashing, his voice ominously low. "Is that what this is? I'll wash, you dry—we brush up against each other while we put stuff away? I'm not interested in that. I've *had* all that, and I don't need it."

"I just wanted something to do while you were—"

"You wanna do something?" He grabbed her shoulders and searched her eyes for some kernel of truth. "What do you wanna do, Mariah? What have you got in mind?"

"Not—"

His kiss was hard and hungry. His hands were warm and wet on her shoulders as he pulled her against him, driving the breath from her lungs while his chest heaved as though he'd suddenly broken into a run. He plunged his tongue past her lips, drew back and plunged again. His hands felt powerful as they kneaded her back, and he slanted his mouth for better access to hers. He took a wider stance, slid his hands over her bottom and fitted himself against her. "Not what?" he whispered against her lips.

"Not this," she gasped.

"Not this what?"

"Not this way." She braced her hands against his chest.

He tightened his hold on her buttocks and held her fast. "How do you want it, then?"

"I don't—"

"What are you doing here?"

"I don't know."

"You're not lost."

"Not anymore," she admitted in a small voice.

"You know damn well this is the way it was before."

"No, it wasn't! It wasn't like this." She took a deep breath, trying to calm herself. She wouldn't let herself be afraid of him. "It's different now."

He saw the defiance in her eyes, and she saw the fury in his. He let her go, and they stepped back, eyeing each other warily.

"You're damn right it's different now. You've got a name. I've got a name. That makes a hell of a difference." He snatched his jacket off the settee, but he didn't bother to put it on as he headed for the door. He was warm enough. "I'll get my own breakfast."

He slammed the door behind him.

Mariah stood there staring at the door and hugging herself, hoping to stop her trembling. Her thudding heart was behaving no differently from the way it had the first time he'd touched her, even though, whether he remembered or not, he'd held her differently that night at Telly's. He had touched her shoulders with a gentle hand and sheltered her in his arms. She'd touched him, too, in other ways—at least, she'd thought she had. There had been that warm soft sheen in his eyes. She remembered every nuance, but he had apparently forgotten.

The sound of bubbling water drew her head around. The water Seth had set on the stove for her bath had come to a boil. Blistering hot, the way he'd touched her. Not the way she wanted him to touch her, but, God, how she wanted to be touched. Dazed, she turned off the stove and made her way to the back room for soap and a towel.

Seth didn't know how far he'd walked before he remembered that he was unarmed and that there was probably a wounded bear in the vicinity. He turned on his heel and started back, telling himself to forget how good she had tasted. She was bad medicine. She had been a mistake, right from the start. He had once allowed himself the luxury of holding her too long, enjoying that sweet satiety and letting himself pretend for a moment that she wasn't just another quick woman. Then he'd permitted himself another moment, and another. Damn, she felt good in his arms. Even tonight. He'd been angry with himself before he even touched her, but beyond the anger, it felt good to hold her. Too good for a quick lay. He had to get that through his thick head.

He was collecting logs from the woodpile before he'd given his intentions much thought. Evidently somewhere deep in his brain he was concerned that she might get cold during the night. He hadn't left her much wood, and she probably wouldn't know that the fire would need a few more logs to keep it going all night. Besides, he'd left the cabin without his rifle. He had his excuse. Now that he'd cooled off a little, he might manage some kind of an apology. The light from the lamp still glowed from the window, so he knew she hadn't gone to bed.

He approached the window and stopped midstride. It was not his intention to spy on her, but he would never have expected to catch her bathing in the front room. His eyes widened, and his mouth went dry. She stood barefoot on the stone hearth, basking in the heat of the fireplace. Her strong calves and tapered, toned thighs looked milky in the lamplight. She had the firm buttocks of an athlete, and his palms itched as he remembered cupping them in his hands.

She reached to dip a white cloth into the pot of water on the stone mantel, then held it to the side of her neck and let the water stream down her long lean back. She'd pinned her hair up, but a few damp, dark tendrils curled at her nape. He longed to see her turn around, and he prayed that she wouldn't. Her hand slid down, and he imagined what he couldn't see—the white cloth cleansing her breast. Her shoulders rose as she took a deep breath. Did they tremble as she exhaled, or was that, too, his imagination?

She bent again, allowing him a glimpse of the soft curve of the underside of her breast. She washed her belly. He could feel the circular motion deep in the pit of his own stomach as her elbow moved back and forth. On the outside looking in, he felt a flush of heat despite the cold night air. Embarrassment, perhaps, but he couldn't drag his eyes from the window. Her skin glistened, and he knew it would feel like warm, wet satin. She didn't appreciate it. He would.

Seth turned abruptly and set his arm load of firewood next to the corner of the cabin. He had his faults, but he was no Peeping Tom. He could do without his rifle tonight. If Mariah got cold toward morning, she knew where to find him.

Chapter Three

In the dim gray light that came before dawn, Seth slipped inside the cabin with an arm load of wood. He closed the door quietly and stood there for a moment wondering how anyone could sleep as soundly as the woman in his bed. She'd tucked herself into her sleeping bag and tossed his blanket over that. Her dark hair spilled over the edges of his pillow. Soft light, cold cabin. He could have been undressed and in that bed beside her in two seconds, easy. The memory of last night, a different shade of soft light, water trickling over burnished skin—that was his to keep. God in heaven, what a vision.

But now he was spying again. He wondered whether he should make more noise and let her know he was there, or just let her sleep. Either way, it wasn't like him to stand around drooling over a woman when she wasn't looking. Not even when she *was* looking. She was probably right, he told himself as he crossed the floor quietly on rubber soles. Lately he'd spent too much time watching the world through a pair of binoculars. After he closed the station down for the winter, he owed himself a week's worth of lively bars and loose women.

He laid the fire carefully, but he heard the bedding rustle and the springs creak when the quick crack of the match woke her. "Temperature really dropped during the night," he said as he watched the flames rise. "I know it's early. I'll get out of here in a minute, and you can go back to sleep."

Mariah checked the buttons on her flannel shirt, then cleared her throat as she sat up. "You want some breakfast?"

"I'll get something later." He closed the airtight door on the fireplace insert as he stood. "The water in the tank should be hot soon."

"You filled it this—" she glanced at the window and yes, you could almost call it "—morning?"

"I've gotta go bear hunting." His tone was joyless, but he turned and discovered a touch of joy in the sight of her bare legs dangling over the side of his bed. She wore a green plaid shirt and thick white wool socks. The combination made him smile. "You can have the whole place to yourself today."

"*All* day?"

He shrugged. "Depends on the bear."

"Maybe I could go with you."

Seth started to shake his head, but another thought came to him. "Are you afraid to be alone?"

"No." She stretched her legs out in front of her and pointed her toes. "I just don't want to sit around here all day. You're going to tell me to stay inside, right?"

"Right. But I can give you a job to do if you want to make yourself useful."

"What?"

"You can man the tower for me."

"That sounds like fun." Mariah hopped off the bed, and her face brightened. "I've never *manned* anything before."

Her infectious smile drew a wink from him. "You let a *man* show you how, you'll do all right. Give you something to tell those little kids about when you decide to get yourself back to school."

"Do you have a camera? I should take some pictures back with me."

"You know how to use a good 35mm?" He watched her disappear into the back room, her shirttail not quite midthigh, and he thought he might like to take a few pictures, too. "Can you handle the lenses?"

"Oh, I think so. Actually, I knew you had a camera. I figured those pictures in the lookout tower must be yours."

"Little sideline." Or so he called it. His free-lance photography was beginning to pay off.

"They're wonderful. Will I be watching for fires up there?"

"You'll be watching for anything. We'll see how observant you are, teach. There's a test at the end."

"Let me make you some breakfast," she called out from the back room. "I'll bet these powdered eggs are delicious scrambled."

"Yeah, they're okay." She could probably make them taste like the real thing if last night's supper was any indication. He had promised himself she wasn't going to do any more cooking, mostly because her cooking tasted so damn good, but he was already firing up the stove and suggesting, "There's canned ham in there, too."

* * *

Mariah decided she could get used to having binoculars permanently affixed to her face if she spent much time this close to the sky. By early afternoon the clouds hung low, but the changing weather seemed to encourage more activity below. Seth had left her a notebook, and she made a note of everything she saw. A pine marten chased a red squirrel up a tree. A gray lynx appeared on the escarpment above the cabin and stretched out to warm his belly against the rock. Mariah attached a 300mm lens to Seth's camera and snapped pictures until the lynx perked his tufted ears, rose on all fours and poised briefly like an athlete mentally rehearsing his move, then jumped up into the trees. A hawk—Mariah couldn't tell what species—circled overhead with wings outstretched. She made another note.

Seth had explained that he was mainly interested in grizzlies, wolves and fires. Of the three, she was least likely to see a wolf, though there had been one unconfirmed sighting in the area in the past year. Seth would report any sightings to the state's Wolf Ecology Project and the Wildlife Service. His own interest was in bears, but he was getting paid for spotting fires. He'd shown her how to use the radio, just in case.

Just in case. "Won't they wonder who's calling?" she'd asked.

"You can tell them you're just a passerby, or simply tell them your name, or you can let it burn." He'd studied her for a moment, and she'd chafed a little under his scrutiny. He had asked her once if she was running from someone, but he didn't ask again. "Just tell them you're calling from Trumpeter Station and that Cantrell is away from his desk at the moment. If you call to report a fire, nobody's gonna be issuing citations or taking names for the gossip columns."

She was praying there would be no fire. The way the clouds were stacking up, she didn't think she'd have to worry. A dark speck of movement in a distant clearing caught her eye, and she peered through the binoculars. It was a black bear, too small for a grizzly. Mariah watched it until it disappeared into the trees, then turned to the map table to try to locate the clearing and make her note. It probably wasn't important. Seth probably saw black bears every day, but she wanted to get everything down. She wanted him to be impressed with her meticulous attention to detail. Taking up the binoculars again, she picked up where she'd left off, moving around the glass perimeter in a clockwise direction. If anything stirred out there, she would know about it.

Seth had been whacked in the face by tall brush all morning, and he was glad his quarry seemed to be headed for higher ground. The bear wasn't leaving the usual signs. He wasn't feeding, wasn't dropping piles of huckleberry scat. The uneven way he bore his weight was evident in the depth of his tracks. He was badly injured. The animal was driven by only one need now, and that was to keep moving, to flee the pain.

Seth followed, taking the high ground. The trees had thinned to a scattering of stubby firs, but the brush grabbed at his knees. He was nearing exhaustion. Since picking up the bear's trail he'd pushed hard, not allowing himself a moment's rest. The bear's unstinting energy was fueled by fright. Seth's perseverance was powered by compassion. The means to end the bear's misery was slung over his shoulder.

The voice of the bawling bear didn't startle him, although he was surprised by the direction from which it came. He'd thought he was running parallel to and on the high side of the bear's trail, but the brush was rustling on the ridge above him. Seth lifted the strap away from his shoulder and swung the semiautomatic rifle off his back. The angry cry that shattered the mountain's tranquility twisted his gut, but nothing raised his hackles quicker than the sound of rustling vegetation above his head.

He released the safety. Even now, long after the weapon had ceased to be the most important tool of his trade, it was like a third arm to him. But he'd made his peace with that. He liked the warm wooden stock of a hunting rifle better than the impersonal composite fiberglass of the M16 he could have sworn he'd cut his teeth on. Whatever it took to get the job done. The more kills you could claim, the sooner they'd give you a couple of days' R and R. But after a while you didn't want the R and R, because you couldn't relax. Nor could you get the adrenaline pumping the way it did in moments like this, when death was just a step away. Limbo. Above him there was a heavy huffing and a crunch of brush near the edge of the ridge. Seth dropped to one knee.

Near the edge. He'd been there. He'd lived there until he didn't think he could live anywhere else.

Come on, bear. The pain's making you crazy. I'll make it quick and clean.

Quick and clean. He'd gotten to the point where everything was quick, nothing was clean, and he'd been damn near crazy.

The big male silvertip rose from the brush like a specter in the sky. The blond fur that covered his back gave his frame a white outline. He had the markings of a Siamese cat. His face was dark with rage, and his one good forepaw, spiked with claws, became a black silhouette against the rocks. His miserable roar proclaimed the horror of the gore-clotted wound in his shoulder and his shattered paw. His fur was matted and crusty, and Seth envisioned the rolling and twisting the great bear had done to try to drive out the thing that was causing his pain. Seth eased the rifle against his shoulder and took aim. The bear bellowed, his white teeth flashing in Seth's sights.

And then, in Seth's mind, the scene changed.

"Shoot me! For the love of God, Cantrell, shoot me."

Black and red. Everything about the spectral figure was black and red, except his eyes. They were human. They were all that was human, even though they rolled wildly, the whites swallowing up the blue irises. The hulking body was charred and battered. Only the eyes were recognizable.

The crack echoed through the trees until the second shot caught up with it. The bear's roar was silenced as the carcass toppled over the edge of the rocky shelf and rolled down the steep grade. Seth came to his feet slowly as he ejected the spent cartridge. Twenty feet below him, a breeze ruffled the dead bear's brown-and-silver fur. Seth wanted to bury the animal. He didn't want anyone else to view this beautiful beast's final indignity. But there wasn't time. Steel-colored thunderheads were rolling in his direction. There was never time to do right by the remains, he told himself. Something always pressed the survivors to move on.

He listened to the rumbling sky while he cut out the poacher's slug and tagged the carcass. There was about fifteen seconds' delay between the flash of lightning and the booming sound of its voice, which meant that very soon he was going to get soaked. He didn't want to be a target for heaven's electricity on this high ridge. He moved quickly, heading for the trees lower down. A crack of lightning struck not far behind him, and he envisioned the lookout tower. He hoped Mariah would seek lower ground, too, and the sooner the better. This weather was headed her way, and he didn't like the idea of her descending those open steps. The thought worried him, and he started jogging just as the deluge came down around his ears.

She's an experienced hiker, he told himself. She'll be fine. But he hadn't decided how much of that he believed, and he wanted to get back to her. The pelting rain stung his face, but he had no thought of taking cover and waiting it out. He skidded down an embankment, loose rocks tumbling after him. The faster he moved, the harder the urgency pounded in his brain.

The storm had looked ominous from the lookout tower. Mariah had decided well before it hit that she was going to weather it closer to the ground. The lightning struck the distant mountain ridges as though it were aiming at select targets, and she prayed that Seth wasn't one of them. Rejecting that notion, she scampered down the steps and hurried back to the cabin ahead of the rain. When Seth came back, she knew he'd appreciate a hot supper.

He could smell it. She had made another miracle with that sundry assortment of cans and plastic packages from the storage room. The aroma of beef and the light in the window greeted him. He was soaked right down to his underwear and stumbling over the gravel, but he was back, and the cabin had never looked so good to him. He rapped on the door and called her name so she wouldn't be startled when he walked in. The place looked even better when the door swung away from his hand and Mariah appeared with her bright, green-eyed smile.

"This storm had me worried," she said.

"Yeah, I know," he answered, puffing as he laid the rifle aside. "When you're this close to the sky, a storm seems to swallow you up. I'm glad you came down from the lookout."

"I was worried about you. That lightning—" There was no need to say more. They looked at one another, and each knew what the other had feared.

Even in her anxiety, there was a lovely softness. He imagined himself pulling her into his arms and letting her know that he was glad to see her. Not a wise move, he warned himself. He'd be getting himself into another exposed position.

The water was running off his hair and puddling on the floor. Bedraggled as he was, she still found him a welcome sight. He smelled of rainwater and pine. "I made beef stew for supper," she said. "I hope it turned out right."

He stripped away his sodden jacket. "Smells like it did."

"It'll keep until you've had a warm shower. I saved the water for you."

The look in her eyes made him forget his soggy underwear for the moment and offer a smile. "You could have used it this afternoon. It would have filled up again by now."

"I didn't think of that."

Again he felt the urge to touch her. "Thanks. I wouldn't mind sharing."

She glanced away. "I made do quite well last night with the water you heated on the stove."

I know was on the tip of his tongue. "I won't be long. I didn't know how hungry I was until I—" She looked up at him again, and he took it all in—the whole sweet picture. Green eyes full of promise, dark brown hair rich with red highlights, and a body under those jeans and that chamois-soft shirt that was as thoroughly fit as it was feminine. "Until I came through that door," he finished quietly.

"I'll take your clothes."

"You'll what?"

"Hand them out to me, and I'll hang them near the fireplace."

He swallowed. "Good idea." He'd done it a hundred times himself. What was he thinking? He pulled a chair away from the table and sat down to wrestle with his wet boots.

"Can I help?"

"No need."

"It's harder when they're wet." She stood in front of him and held out her hands for his foot. "I think I might have seen a wolf today," she said, her tone hopeful.

He eyed her for a moment, then raised his leg and let her take his boot heel in her hands. "What makes you think so?"

"You have a picture of coyotes up there, and there's that book on wolves. I got a good look at him. It was right before the storm, and he was sniffing the air as though he were gauging its approach." She took a wide stance and pulled up on his heel. "I think he was too big to be a coyote."

He wiggled his foot inside the boot, which looked absurdly large in her small hands. "Where did you see him?"

"I took notes on everything," she reported. "The wolf was just east of the tower. All of a sudden, there he was on that little ridge. He was beautiful."

"I'll bet."

"You don't believe me."

"I believe you think you saw a wolf, but I know the chances that it *was* a wolf are pretty slim." She looked like the child whose balloon had burst. He felt as though he were the guy with the pin. "Coyotes can get pretty big sometimes," he offered.

"I know what a coyote looks like." The boot slid free, and she bobbled backward. He reached for her, but she caught her balance and dropped the boot onto the floor. "I think I saw a wolf."

"We'll call it an unconfirmed sighting." He peeled off his wet sock before he gave her his other foot. She bent over to get a good grip, and her shirt drooped enough to offer him a glimpse of the valley between her breasts.

"Who has to confirm it?" she asked.

"I do." He wanted to confirm a few other things right now. Like whether that valley was still as soft as he remembered.

"Fat—" she pulled the boot off with one mighty tug "—chance."

"Hey, I give credit where it's due. I'll keep an eye out."

"Did you find the bear?"

"Yeah."

"You got him, then?"

"Yeah, I got him."

The second boot dropped to the floor with a thud. "Good. I'm tired of being locked up inside."

"You ever seen a grizzly?" With a wet sock dangling from his fingers, he braced his hands on his knees and stared her down. "I don't mean in a zoo. I mean wild and roaming free."

"I saw a black bear today."

"I want you to see a grizzly." He stood abruptly and

tossed the sock atop his boots, as if its condition disgusted him. "Then we'll see how easily you say, 'Good,' because I killed him."

"I didn't mean that it was—" He had already disappeared into the storage room. Mariah stood near the door, which Seth hadn't quite closed, and stared at the doorknob. She hadn't meant that she *wanted* the bear dead.

He thrust a wad of wet clothes through the crack in the door. "Here."

She took the jeans and shirt from his hand. "Is that all?"

"What else do you want?"

"Whatever's wet."

"Everything back here is wet, including me. I'll be out in a minute."

The splash of the shower joined the steady patter of rain on the shingled roof. As she set the table for supper, Mariah promised herself that this was going to be a pleasant evening. She would see to it. She would set the tone, and she would get him to talk. She'd come up here with an agenda in mind, and she was going to accomplish at least part of it. When she left, he would no longer be a stranger.

Seth emerged from the back room wearing jeans and a red flannel shirt, which he neglected to button. His dark hair had been toweled, and he raked his fingers through it in a one-shot attempt to manage it as he pulled the door shut behind him. "Let's move that table closer to the fire," he suggested. "God, it's cold back there."

"I hope you didn't get chilled," she offered as she turned from the stove.

"Hell, I'm chilled to the marrow, but I'll get over it. Let's get this—" He indicated her end of the table with a gesture while he took a grip on the opposite side. "Now

I'll find some dry socks, and we'll be in business. Are you gonna be too hot over there?''

"No, this is fine." Maternally confident that she had prepared the perfect cure for him, she took the bowls from the table. "What you need is some hot stew."

"Yeah." He padded across the room on bare feet and dragged a wooden box from under the bed. "This is where I keep underwear and socks, in case you run out."

The offer made her laugh as she imagined herself wearing a pair of his briefs.

He looked up, grinning. "Well, you never know."

"I can always hand wash my own."

He sat on the edge of the bed and crossed his ankle over his knee as he unrolled a pair of black wool socks. "Just trying to be a good host. What's mine is yours."

"I'll keep that in mind."

She was dishing up the stew, and his stomach reacted audibly. He pulled the socks on quickly and joined her at the table, taking the seat she'd left for him closest to the fireplace. She had even made skillet biscuits. "Where did you learn to cook like this?" He tasted the stew, and she waited for his response to the real test. "This can't be that canned beef," he said. She smiled, her eyes bright with the pleasure of having pleased him. "This is great, Mariah."

He spoke her name naturally, as though it had been part of his life for some time. Another step away from anonymity, she thought. "My mother died when I was twelve. I've been cooking for a long time."

He raised an eyebrow in surprise. "You've been doing all the cooking in your family since you were twelve?"

"A lot of it. Dad and I kind of fumbled along for a while, but I got to be pretty good at it."

"No brothers or sisters?"

"No. Just my father and me."

Something about the way she strained to put those words together disturbed him. "What does your dad do now that you're on your own?"

"He's a car dealer," she said, skirting the issue. But she felt a need to tell him more. "He also takes a very active interest in my skiing."

Which Seth realized *he* hadn't done so far. "What kind of skiing do you do?"

"Cross-country. I compete—" No, that wasn't the important part. Why had she thrown that in right away? "Sometimes."

"Seems like a combination that would be hard to juggle—skiing and teaching. They're both winter sports."

"Teaching is hardly a sport." Mariah's spoon rested in her bowl, all but forgotten. "I only taught part-time last year, and I told you, this year I took a leave of absence. I hope to be able to substitute in the spring and maybe go full time next year. My school board has been patient because—" Because of who she was and who her father was. Hometown athlete. Successful local businessman. In Bozeman, Montana, Mariah Crawford and her father were held in high esteem. "Well, because they *say* they want me on their staff."

"Don't you believe them?"

"Yes, of course," she said a little too quickly. "I'm a good teacher."

"So who pays the bills?" Seth eyed her expectantly as he broke open a warm biscuit. Moist crumbs fell into his palms. "Daddy?"

She poked at a piece of meat with her spoon. "He pays quite a few of them, yes."

"And that has something to do with this time you needed to spend alone?"

"That's part of it. My father was a terrific Alpine skier, but he took a bad fall years ago, so he gave it up in favor of Nordic skiing—what most people call cross-country. When he started including me, I took to it like a kid to candy."

The tension melted from her shoulders, and her face became remarkably serene. "I loved to ski. I loved to be outdoors in winter, not at busy resorts, necessarily, but in beautiful country like this, making my own tracks in a couple of inches of fresh snow. I got strong. I developed a good, powerful stride because I'm persistent. That's one good thing about me—I don't give up," she declared. It almost sounded like a sales pitch. "If I decide I want to do something, really *do* it, I'll put in the time and effort to do it right."

"I believe you," he assured her with a smile. But he wondered whether this was Mariah or her father talking.

"Then we got into the amateur racing routine, collegiate competition, and now—" She lowered her eyes and began prodding at her stew again. "Well, I still love to ski, but I don't think it has to be the end of the world if I don't make the Olympic trials."

"And your dad does," he concluded around a mouthful of biscuit.

"He thinks it's the chance of a lifetime—that it'll never come again."

"The Olympics only come around every four years."

"Yes, but what if that schedule just doesn't fit into mine? What if I'm not…ready?"

"Then you don't make it," Seth said with an easy shrug. "But if you've got a shot at it, why not take it?"

"Because there are other things that are more important."

"Eating obviously isn't one of them."

"I'm eating." One spoonful of beef almost made it to her mouth. "But, you know…there *are* other things."

"Like your teaching?"

"Yes, that's one of them."

He watched her put the spoon into her mouth, and he said a mental *thank you*, telling himself he didn't like to see food wasted. Or time. Or people's lives. The solution to the competition business was obvious.

"Then tell your dad to strap on the skis and try out for the team himself."

"It isn't that simple. He's put a lot of time and effort, a lot of money, a lot of his *life*, into this thing."

There they were—time and life. But she was talking about her father's. "If you're a world-class skier, you must have put a lot of your time into it, too. It's *your* life, isn't it?"

"I don't know." She wanted it to be her life. For years, there was nothing else she'd wanted more. But her father was right; she'd come this far. She was *this* close. And he wanted it so badly. She could see it in her father's eyes every time she looked at him.

But now she was looking at Seth, and what she saw in his seemed to reflect an open mind. "Other people's lives overlap ours, and ours overlap theirs," she said. "When is it okay to say, 'This much of me is mine, and this is what I'm going to do with it'?"

"Whenever you decide." He propped his elbows on the table and dangled his spoon above the remains of his stew as he spoke. "I'd say you've got a problem with deciding what you really want. You said you're taking a leave of absence. That means you've got a bunch of time on your hands with nothing to do except go to parties, hike around where you're not safe, or get yourself in shape and ski. You've already put your teaching on hold.''

''You think I should go through with it, then?''

''I don't think you should do anything. I'm just making an observation, and I don't even know why I'm doing that. What business is it of mine?''

''I'd like to think that…if you were a friend…''

''If I were a friend?'' He drew his face into a scowl. ''How well do you know your friends?''

''I can't say that I have many.'' It sounded like a bid for sympathy, so she hastened to add, ''I just haven't had time.''

''So, what's this?'' He spread his hands apart with the question. ''You're making time for me. I'm not much of a friend to too many people.''

''I think you could be,'' she suggested quietly.

''You think if I were a friend, it would be a whole lot easier. This whole thing would be a whole lot easier— you and me and what's already gone down. Well, it wouldn't. It'd be a damn sight stickier than it already is.''

He saw the hurt in her eyes. Women could dig up that look at the drop of a hat when a man was just trying to be honest. He felt crawly inside. ''Look, I'm not trying to be some kind of a cocky bastard. I'm just saying I'm in no position to give you any advice about what to do with your life. I understand bears better than I do people.''

Mariah nodded as she forced her attention to her food. The stew had gotten cold, but she took a bite anyway. She chewed slowly as she studied her bowl. Fat particles floated like bits of paraffin in the brown gravy. She steeled herself and took another bite.

Seth clamped his teeth together, hoping his considerable patience wouldn't explode. *Damn*, she ate that stuff as if it were a huge wad of gum.

At last she swallowed and looked up from her bowl. "I'm sorry about the bear."

"What?"

"I'm sorry you had to shoot that bear."

"Yeah." It was Seth's turn to find something else to look at. He reached for his coffee. "I am, too."

"Was he hurt really bad?" Without taking his eyes off his coffee mug, Seth nodded. "Then you had no choice. It was the only merciful thing to do."

"Yeah. The merciful thing."

Mariah reached across the table, laid her hand on Seth's arm and waited for him to look up at her. "The man who shot him first was his killer," she said. "Not you. What I said about being stuck in the cabin…I didn't mean that the way it sounded." His expression was vacant, and she was sure he was unconvinced. "What will you do about the poacher?"

"He's probably long gone by now. I reported it last night, but I guess there's a fire in the southern part of the state. They told me to hold down the fort for another couple of days."

She pulled her hand back across the table. "Did you say anything about me?"

"No, and neither did they." He eyed her more thoughtfully now. "Which either means you didn't leave anybody a clue about where you were going, or you do this all the time, and nobody thinks anything of it."

Telly had all the clues, and she was the one friend her father knew nothing about. She *did* have one friend, Mariah thought with satisfaction.

"Why didn't you report me?" she asked.

He finally permitted himself to smile. "I may not be

much of a friend, but I never was much of a squealer, either. You'll go back when the chopper comes, no big deal.''

"Really?"

"Well, it isn't every day a woman wanders into my station—that's a big deal—but we'll handle it quietly. I assume that's what you want.''

"Yes." She glanced at the fireplace. "Have you gotten warmed up yet?"

"The stew helped. It was delicious." He sipped his coffee, hoping that would help, too. "I can't quite shake that soggy underwear feeling. I have a long-standing aversion to being wet all the way through, but I'm always miles from anywhere when the rain comes.''

"With a job like yours, I guess it comes with the territory." He'd let her shift the focus to himself, and she wanted to see how long that might last. "Have you always been a ranger?"

"No." Okay, so it was his turn. Not to run off at the mouth, but to say something. She *had* asked nicely. "I was a kid once. But I was hell-bent on becoming a man, so I enlisted in the marines and did a couple of hitches in 'Nam.''

"That did it?"

"Got rid of the kid, anyway. I don't know what kind of a man it made me, but I acquired some rather specialized skills. So later on, a few years down the road, I figured, soldier, ranger—sounded close enough.''

It sounded too simple, but she thought he might tell her more in his own time if she didn't press him. "When were you married?"

"Married?"

"You got mad at me over the dishes last night. You said you'd had it with the domestic scene.''

"Oh, yeah. I did get pretty snarly, didn't I?" He sipped again and decided this was something she had a right to know, considering. "Yeah, I was married once. Had a wife, but couldn't keep her." *Had a wife, but scared the hell out of her.*

"Did you have any children?"

"No. No children." He remembered a time when he'd wanted a child, but Carla, his wife, had been quick to point out that a man like him wouldn't have made a good father. "What a disaster that would have been."

His dark tone left a hollow ring in Mariah's ears. Clearly Seth wanted no ties. Still, he was revealing little bits of himself. She saw herself as a gleaner, snatching up each kernel and tucking it away, keeping the promise she'd made to herself that he would not be a stranger to her when they parted company this time.

He made no move to help her with the dishes. Instead, he tossed more wood on the fire, pushed the hand-hewn settee closer and basked in the heat in silence. He was shivering on the inside, and he was beginning to admit to himself that it had nothing to do with wet underwear. When Mariah moved to join him, she found him hugging himself and staring into the flames.

"Shouldn't we close the door?" she asked, indicating the fireplace insert.

"No. Leave it." He clamped his jaw against further explanation. He would lose control if he talked.

He looked strange, a little pale and glassy eyed, Mariah thought. "Are you all right?"

"Could you get me something—" He steadied his molars against each other for a moment, then tried again. "Maybe something hot to drink?"

"You really *are* chilled, aren't you?" She dragged the Indian-print wool blanket off the bed and brought it to him. His arms were fastened around his middle like a corset, his hands wedged under his armpits, and he made no move to take the blanket. Mariah sat beside him and spread it over him, tucking the edge of it under his chin. "Do you feel sick?"

"Yeah." That did it. His teeth were clacking like some windup practical joke. "It's n-nothing n-new. I'll be okay in a f-few hours."

"You've had this before?" He nodded briefly. "What is it?"

"M-malaria. I st-still get relapse-ses."

"Since Vietnam?"

He gave his head a quick shake. "Central Americ-ca. D-do s-something for me?"

She edged closer. "What can I do?"

"Got s-some p-pills."

"Where?"

"Under the b-bed."

"Where you keep your socks?"

He nodded again. She tucked the blanket around his shoulders and dashed to the bed to pull out the box, then the bottle. "Is this it? Chloroquine?" She interpreted his grunt as an affirmative response and returned with the medication and a glass of water. His hand trembled so badly that she had to steady the glass and help him drink.

"You should be in bed, Seth."

"T-too c-cold."

"Will this last all night?" His teeth chattered loudly as he nodded. "What else do you...how can I help?"

"Just k-keep me warm."

Chapter Four

Mariah decided to move the furniture. If Seth wouldn't go to bed, she would bring the bed to Seth. The clatter of his teeth gave her sympathetic chills as she shoved the settee out of the way and pushed the bed closer to the fireplace. She fussed over the bedding and rearranged her sleeping bag. She'd keep him warm, and she'd make him comfortable.

Seth huddled in his blanket in a corner chair and watched Mariah's maneuverings. He'd weathered this storm alone just fine before. He told himself he ought to order her to bed so he could be miserable without an audience, but issuing orders in his condition was pretty useless. He knew that from experience. It was a little like drinking a whole quart of that rotgut tequila they used to get sometimes south of the border. After a bout with malaria, he could find himself missing a whole day and wondering what in hell he'd said and done in front of whoever happened to be hanging around his bed. A squad of rebels. Some native witch doctor. Carla.

Mariah. He pulled the blanket tighter around his body and watched her toss back the covers and turn to him. She was bound and determined to get him into that bed. God, she was beautiful. Her skin glowed with a milky sheen, so brightly that she burned his eyes.

"You want me to carry you?" she challenged.

He gave her what he believed was a smile.

"You don't think I can?"

"I don't think you c-can," he mumbled as he heaved himself out of the chair. "But you might give it a hummiliating sh-shot." He tottered, but she was there to steady him.

"What happens now?" she asked. "Do you throw up?"

"You want me to s-spoil all the surprises?"

"I want to be ready for them." She knew he was trying not to lean heavily on her, but he seemed to have lost his equilibrium.

"I don't want you to—" He crawled into bed, and Mariah helped him take off his jeans before she covered him with the puffy sleeping bag and his blankets. "Damn, I'm sorry," he said with a groan. "Helluva way…treat a guest."

"Don't worry." She sat beside him and touched his face. His teeth had stopped chattering, and, Lord, he was burning up. "I teach six-year-olds. They throw up on me all the time."

"Like hell." He closed his eyes, hating this weakness. "If I talk out of my head…ignore it, okay?"

"Okay," she whispered. Tentatively she stroked his hair. "How bad does the fever get?"

"Bad. 'S okay. Goes away."

"Can I get you anything?"

He rolled his head from side to side. "Just don't you...go away."

She smiled. "Are you talking out of your head yet?"

He offered a slight smile in blind response to the one he heard in her voice, but he kept his eyes closed. "Probably. I'm sick, so humor me."

"I'm not going anywhere," she promised.

While Seth slept Mariah showered. The rain had refilled the cistern. The cool water provided a relief from the roaring fire, and its natural softness made her hair feel silky, even when it was wet. She dressed in one of Seth's flannel shirts because it covered more of her than hers did, and because he'd offered the use of his clothes, but mostly just because it was his. It was a small claim to make on him.

His tortured groan brought her back to his bedside. He had thrown back the blankets, but he offered little resistance when she covered him again. His skin felt terribly hot, and his lips were dry. He was panting as though he'd been running, but he took only a taste of the water she offered him.

"Are you in pain?" she asked.

"My head aches." It was a gross understatement. The pain was so bad it blurred his vision.

"Can you take aspirin?"

"Aspirin won't touch it."

"In another couple of hours you're supposed to get more pills, according to the directions on the bottle."

He nodded. She really wanted to help; he could see that, albeit dimly, in the way she looked him. The blue shirt looked like one of his. He reached up to touch it, and his hand slid along her arm. He was as weak as a kitten, and he didn't mean to brush his knuckles against the side of her breast.

Yeah, he did. It was nice. "Shirt looks good on you," he said.

"I just thought—"

"You been out in the rain?" He scowled, trying to focus better. "Your hair looks wet." He touched the silky ends and confirmed his suspicions.

"I washed it."

"Careful when you go outside," he muttered. "Can't look after you now. Want you here…safe…with me."

"Okay." She smiled at him again, even though his eyes were closed. With his tousled black hair and his hard, square jaw he looked dangerously appealing. She assured him, "I'll be careful."

"Touch my face again." Seth's voice sounded scratchy, but still his request took Mariah's breath away. She hesitated. She risked such heartache with each intimacy she indulged. What chance was there for her to take care of herself while she was caring for him? She touched his chin with her thumb, then laid her hand along the side of his face.

"Feels so cool," he said.

She moved to the place where a headboard might have been and knelt on the floor.

"Don't go," he implored.

She leaned close to his ear and whispered, "I'm here. I won't go." She pressed her fingertips against his temples and rotated them slowly while she stroked his forehead with her thumbs. "Tell me if this helps."

"It helps." He wanted her hands on him, and the illness gave him an excuse to indulge himself. He felt as though someone were hammering on the walls inside his head, so he concentrated on the strokes that soothed over him on the outside.

He lost himself for a while, but then he felt her shift her weight. "Getting tired?"

"No, no. I'm fine." Her nose was inches from the top of his head, and she could smell the balsam-scented shampoo he'd used earlier. She wanted to feel his hair against her face.

"Come to bed," he suggested quietly.

"I thought I'd sleep—"

"Here. With me." He took her hand from his face and held it in his. "Keep me warm."

"You're as hot as a firebrick," she said.

"Lie beside me, then. I'll warm you."

She didn't question the invitation. It put her where she wanted to be, at least at that moment. She slipped under the covers on the side of the bed opposite the fire. He didn't reach for her, nor did she cuddle up to him, but she drifted to sleep in a cocoon made warm by his body. Her tender comfort helped him hold back the pain as he hovered near delirium's edge. Always near the edge.

"For God's sake, get down!"

Mariah's head popped up from the pillow, but she was knocked back down by what felt like a fiery log.

"Keep your head down, you dumb little bastard," Seth grumbled.

Mariah's eyes widened in the near darkness. Seth puffed as though he'd been mountain climbing. "What is it?" she whispered. He groaned. "Seth, are you—" His arm was a leaden weight across her neck. She slid both hands underneath it and tried to ease it away. Her jaw hurt. He was only flailing around, she told herself. He hadn't meant to hit her. But his strength scared her. "Can you hear me, Seth?"

"Tracers," he mumbled.

"No, it's okay. You're safe. You're in your bed. It's only a dream." She turned to her side as she tried to reach for him, but he grabbed her arm. Her eyes adjusted to the waning firelight, and she saw his wild-eyed stare.

"Oh, Lord, I slept through the time for your medication."

"Had to shoot him," he whispered desperately. "He was hurt bad."

"I know." She shrugged out of his grasp and scooted closer, trying to touch his face.

He snatched her hand and squeezed it tightly. "Blood everywhere."

"I know." She was braced on her elbow, and he had her other hand, but she was determined to touch him somehow. She stretched her neck and slid her cheek against his. So feverish, she thought, and he hadn't broken into a sweat. "It's all right, Seth," she whispered near his ear. "It's all over."

"He doesn't…want anyone to see him like that."

"They won't," she promised.

"Cool," he muttered. "Cool and soft."

"That's what you need." She drew back a little. "I'll get your pills and try to bring the fever down with—"

"Where the hell…" His expression hardened, and he jerked on her arm. "Where do you think you're going?"

"I'm going to—"

"Who were you with?" he barked.

"No one…*you*, just you."

"You've been with him, haven't you?"

His eyes were filled with pain, and she wasn't sure how much was physical and how much mental. "I'll be right back, Seth." She sat up slowly, and he let her move his hand from her arm. "You need those pills to make you better."

He sighed and fell back against the pillow. "Get the hell out, then," he muttered as he passed his hand over his eyes. "Who needs you? Who the hell...needs you, anyway?"

He'd looked at her and seen someone else. Why not? Mariah thought as she held a match to the wick of a kerosene lantern. They had passed through each other's lives one night, and she had meant nothing to him. The important pieces of his life were jumbled in his brain right now, and his former wife, not Mariah, was one of them.

But Mariah was there, and it was she who would take him his pills and sponge his fever-ridden body. He had given her something precious on his way through her life that night. He'd stopped for a moment to hold her when she had needed more than anything to be held. Tonight it was her turn.

She returned to the bed, slipped her arm beneath his head and pressed two pills between his dry lips. "Can you swallow these, Seth? Take some water."

His eyelids fluttered, and he took pains to look up at her. Then he moved his jaw, and she heard him crush the pills between his teeth. His lips parted for the glass.

"I'm going to bathe you," she promised. "Here, in bed. It'll feel good to you. It'll cool you. But I want to get a nice slow-burning fire going first so you won't get chilled. Okay?"

When he gave no indication of understanding, she eased him back down and took care of the fire. She came back with a basin of water and a soft cloth. His eyes glistened as he watched her bunch the blankets below his waist and unbutton his shirt, but he said nothing. She slipped the shirt from his arms and left it under him to catch the water.

She started with his face and worked her way down. His chest and shoulders were beautifully contoured with hard muscle, and she followed each curve with her cloth. He was a tough man, but there was tenderness, too. She had enjoyed his tenderness that first night. Now she knew more. Like the image in his hallucination, he would not have wanted her to see him this way. He would not have chosen to let her see the part of him that was so tender, so sore that it needed protection. She cleansed him gently.

"Your hands are what feels the best."

She glanced up, surprised by the butter-soft sound of his voice. His breathing was rapid and shallow, but his voice was steadier than it had been since the onset of the fever.

"Do you know who I am?" she asked.

"Mariah."

She smiled. "Yes."

"Mariah Crawford. Crawford's Mountain."

"You made that up."

"Somebody made up Pike's Peak."

She laid her palm against the side of his face. "Are you feeling any better?"

"I will be by morning," he promised.

"Do you remember saying—"

He shook his head. "You promised to ignore whatever I said tonight."

"Even now?"

"Especially now." He lifted her hand and placed her palm over his lips. They were warm, but they made her shiver. He knew. He smiled and put her hand in the center of his chest. She felt the rapid tattoo of his heartbeat, and she closed her eyes, letting it record itself on her hand. "Nobody's ever done anything like this for me before," he told her.

She knew full well, but she asked anyway. "Like what?"

"Tended me like this."

She wanted to ask about his wife, but she looked at him lovingly and asked instead, "Why not?"

"I always...I hate being weak like this."

"You're ill. You're not weak."

"Times like this I...I never wanted anyone near me."

"You had no choice this time."

He shook his head. "I wanted you near me...*want* you...want you here."

"I am here."

He raised his hands to the front of her shirt.

"Seth—"

He slipped the first button through the buttonhole.

She was suddenly short of breath. "Seth, I don't think—"

"I won't try to... It's just that...you've been touching me a lot."

"I couldn't help it," she offered weakly.

"I can't, either." He fumbled with the third button, and finally it came loose. "I just want to put my face..."

"Oh, Seth, don't..."

Two more buttons came free. He crumpled handfuls of the open shirt and used it to bring her closer to him. Between her breasts she felt his heat, his breath, then every detail of his face—his smooth forehead, his eyelids, his nose, his stubbled cheeks. Her nipples tightened in response. The cloth she'd used to bathe him fell to the floor, and she rolled to her side and cradled his head in her arms.

"You feel so good," he whispered. "So smooth and cool."

"You might use my name while you're passing out this praise, just so I know you're not hallucinating."

"Mariah," he whispered hotly. "Like the wind."

There *was* a wind. It rustled the pines and swept the rain against the door. It was a cold sound. But his breath came like a hot breeze through the valley of her breasts. Nothing they'd shared had seemed as intimate as this embrace, and she cherished it. Later she would remember the texture and tone of every word, and she would remember how they had kept the lonely wind at bay.

"Will it help you sleep if I hold you this way?" she asked.

"It can't hurt. You have the nicest...prettiest..."

She rotated her thumb against his temple and stroked his hair, and soon they both drifted to sleep with the patter of the rain.

She woke in a puddle, and she thought the roof must have leaked. Then she realized that Seth had broken into a drenching sweat. Oh, God, he'd gotten worse. She hurried to find a towel and get some more water.

"What's wrong?" he managed groggily when she began washing his body again.

"You're all in a sweat, Seth," she complained as she mopped his face. "It must be getting worse."

He lay there watching her and wondering why he was suffering all these frantic ministrations. He could just as well take the cloth from her and do this himself. But, of course, he didn't. He was sick, not crazy.

"What are you smiling about?" Mariah demanded. "I don't know what else to do. I think we'd better radio your headquarters or whatever and tell them you need medical attention. I've tried everything I can think of."

"I know. That's why I'm smiling."

"Well, I fail to see the humor. I think you're very, very sick, and I'm sca—"

They looked at each other. Seth's smile faded as the word formed itself in both their minds. "Scared?" he asked quietly.

"You're *sick*."

And she *was* scared. *For him.*

"It always happens like this," he said after several long seconds of silence. "The fever's broken now. I'll be okay in a few hours."

She sighed, her shoulders dropping with relief. "I was afraid the medication wasn't doing any good."

"You're doing some good." He took her hand, which still held the cloth, and pressed it against his chest. "It feels good when you bathe the sweat away."

She moved slowly at first. It took a moment for her anxiety to diminish, and then she realized that he was staring at—she glanced down—her breasts. With her free hand she pulled the shirt together.

"What's that for?" he asked. His smile danced in his eyes. "A little while ago you let me sleep there."

She maneuvered a button with one hand. "A little while ago you were delirious with fever."

"I knew you, though."

"Not entirely."

"I knew you once…entirely."

"Well, that was different, as you've so aptly pointed out. We aren't…strangers anymore."

"No, we aren't." She had touched him differently. She was *still* touching him differently, and, Lord, how it made him ache inside.

"And now that you've got this thing whipped, we… we shouldn't…" She finished her buttoning and took a quick swipe at drying him with the towel. "Turn over and let me do your back," she said quickly as she dipped her cloth into the water again.

"I don't remember cussing you out or anything." He was still feeling shaky as he rolled over. "What personal secrets did I give away?"

"I think you thought I was your wife."

"Oh, yeah?" He sighed with disgust. "During the honeymoon, or after it was over?"

"I wouldn't say you were remembering good times."

"Great." There had been precious few good times to remember, and he thought he'd managed to forget the whole thing. "Just forget whatever I said, okay? It was all fever talk."

"Okay." There were other things she wanted to ask about—other things he'd said—but she was afraid he might try to take them away. She wouldn't let him. She would keep them for herself, protecting them by asking about something else. "Does this happen to you very often?"

"Not like it used to. A couple of times a year. They say it eventually burns itself out."

"That's good news."

"Yeah." He didn't sound convinced. He was still thinking about Carla. The relapses had been worse then, and she used to leave him to sweat it out on his own. She said he got too crazy. Finally she'd told him that he was just crazy *period*, and she'd left him.

"I didn't...say anything real ugly to you, did I?"

"No."

"I didn't mean it if I did."

"It was as though you were having bad dreams," she told him. "I knew you weren't talking to me."

He thought that over. Then, before he knew what he

was about, he found himself confiding, "I get those sometimes without the fever."

"About Vietnam?"

"Yeah. Sometimes."

"That was a long time ago."

"Yeah, well, sometimes...in my mind it seems like..." He wanted to tell her. She wouldn't understand, but he wanted to tell her anyway. She would think he was crazy, too. Damn, he was a fool. "You remember things you'd rather forget," he said, opting for vagueness. "It's stupid."

"I don't think it's stupid. I'm sure it's very painful."

"No, it's stupid. Take my word for it."

She dried his back, straightened the bed up a little and brought him a clean shirt. The word *stupid* echoed in her head. That was exactly what she was being, waiting on him like this. It brought them too close. "I think I'll try the settee now," she decided.

Before she could move away, he caught her hand. "You need rest, Mariah, and you won't get it on that thing. I'll keep my hands to myself. I promise."

"It isn't—"

"Don't tell me what it isn't," he snapped. Wrong tone. He took a deep breath and tugged on her hand. "Just come to bed."

"The fire needs—"

"It'll burn 'til morning, and so will I." He offered a tentative smile. "Come on. We'll be okay."

We'll be okay. It was an enigmatic promise, but she decided to accept it, whatever it meant. We'll be warm enough, she projected as she slid beneath the covers. We'll be sensible. We'll watch our step this time. We'll be okay. We won't do anything crazy, because there's obviously no future in it.

But they already had.

Mariah got up early, and Seth lingered in bed. He said he wasn't interested in food, and she didn't press him. She tried to find some business to be about. The weather had cleared, so she made a trip up to the tower and had a look around. After that she picked up an arm load of wood that had been sheltered under the cabin's eaves and returned to find that Seth's interest in food had been revived.

"How about a hike this morning?" he asked cheerfully between bites of leftover stew.

"Are you up to it?"

"You bet. How 'bout you?"

"Up or down?"

"Thought we'd try Crawford's Mountain." He liked the way she smiled. It made him feel as though he'd actually given her something. "We might see some bighorns up there."

"Oh, I'd love to see some bighorn sheep!"

His smile faded as Mariah approached the table. The chair legs scraped against the floorboards as he came to his feet abruptly. Taking her chin in his hand, he turned her face toward the light. The purpling bruise along her jaw made him sick to his stomach. "I did this, didn't I?"

"You were—" She could just see his eyes out of the corners of hers. They glittered with apparent anger. "I think you were trying to protect me."

"From what?"

"You were dreaming," she reminded him quietly.

"Hallucinating," he said disgustedly. "The only thing you needed protection from was me." He touched the bruise lightly with his thumb, then lowered his hand and his voice. "I'm sorry."

"You never meant to hurt me."

"I should have kept to myself," he said. He picked up his bowl from the table, held the spoon to one side and drained the rest of the stew. "Have something to eat before we go," he instructed, his tone flat.

Seth remembered that his pace had tired Mariah the last time, and she was mindful of his illness. Neither of them was anxious to push the other to physical exhaustion, so they stopped now and then to admire a new overlook, pick huckleberries or spy on a pair of scavenging squirrels. There was little conversation at first as they mulled over their concerns. The hike eventually took them high above the timberline to Alpine meadows within view of steep rocky cliffs.

A sudden, loud *clack* reverberated among the rocks.

"Bingo." Seth's boot heels skidded in the gravel as he stopped to tune in to his sense of direction. No more brooding. The wilderness didn't brood. "C'mon," he said, taking Mariah by the hand. "I'll bet they've saved us ringside seats."

They rounded an outcrop and found themselves conveniently downwind of a bighorn battle. Seth eased his camera from the case. A quick glance at Mariah told him she was all eyes and ears. He began clicking off shots.

Two brown rams with massive full-curl horns backed away from each other and positioned themselves for another charge. Without any perceptible signal they reared simultaneously, then catapulted themselves toward a midair, head-on collision. In the final second they both dropped their hind legs, adding the force of gravity to the bone-jarring impact. Crash! The shock waves rippled from the point of contact across their backs, shaking the dust from their dun coats. Unscathed, the two raised their heads from the clash, turned to the side and played the preening male as they displayed their mighty horns to each other. Viewers—a cluster of ewes at one end and a human couple at the other—saw the flash of their stark white rumps. Moments later the rams were at it again.

"It's a wonder they don't knock each other out," Mariah said quietly.

"Their heads are built for this," Seth explained, his face still behind the camera. "Double-layered skulls, thick hide on their faces, and their heads can pivot and recoil like heavy-duty shock absorbers. They can go on like this for hours."

"Pretty rough game."

"Hardly a game. This is serious high-stakes business. The winner gets to be king of the hill and rut all he wants." Seth chuckled and glanced at Mariah, his eyes twinkling. "All for the love of ewe."

Mariah groaned, then nodded toward the females. "*They* don't look too impressed."

"They probably hear 'ewe' jokes all the time."

"They're probably hoping that handsome stud up there on the hill will make his bid." Mariah pointed to a higher cliff face, and Seth aimed his lens in that direction. There stood a ram whose horns had yet to reach full curl, but he had a deep barrel chest, rich brown coat and regal bearing.

"He'll get his chance," Seth assured her as he snapped a picture. He lowered the camera and stood back just to admire, to assess the animal's potential. "Give him another year."

From Mariah's vantage point, the young ram stood just beyond Seth's rugged profile. She watched the breeze lift Seth's hair and the warm sun burnish the contours of his face. He was as much at home in this high country as the bighorn ram was, Mariah thought, and perhaps he knew the same restiveness.

A sharp crack sounded, echoing from peak to peak. The sheep bolted in several directions as Seth grabbed Mariah by the shoulders and shoved her to the ground, knocking the breath from her lungs. He dropped his body over hers just as it dawned on her what the sound was. Rifle fire.

A second shot rang out. Seth shoved Mariah toward the base of the outcrop, keeping her covered as they moved. She struggled to catch her breath, scrambling in an effort to aid Seth's cause.

"You okay?" he asked when he had her pinned against the rock wall. She nodded, gasping. "The season hasn't opened yet. I don't know whether he's after the sheep or—" He pulled her face around and made her look him in the eye. "I'm asking you again, Mariah. Is somebody after you?"

"Somebody—" The import of his question dawned as sluggishly as her awareness of danger. "They're not shooting at *me*, Seth. I'm just a—" She shook her head vigorously. "No. No one would have any reason to—"

"Okay, okay," he said, releasing her chin. "Poachers again. We'll wait a few minutes before we hightail it out of here."

Moments passed. They heard nothing but the wind and their own unsteady breathing. Seth sat up and turned his binoculars in the direction from which the shots had been fired. "He must've moved on," he concluded after making his survey. He gave Mariah a reassuring look, then helped her to her feet.

They made their way quickly down the barren mountainside. Seth was relieved when they reached the timberline and the safety of cover. He chose a steeper, more direct route than the one they'd used on the climb, and he noticed that someone had broken a trail before them.

"Lot of activity on Crawford's Mountain today," he grumbled. "You didn't invite anyone for a christening, did you?"

"That noise up there wasn't exactly the smashing of a champagne bottle."

"Well, we've sure got ourselves some company."

"Pretty rude company, if you ask me."

Seth jumped down from a five-foot precipice and started to reach for Mariah when something in the trees below caught his eye. He dropped into a crouch and peered through the timber. "Would you look at this?"

He was talking to himself, but Mariah sat on the ledge, swung her legs down and got ready to push off for what she hoped would be an easy landing. He turned in time to stand and catch her. "Looks like somebody's up here playing army," Seth told her as they gained their balance. "There's a camouflaged camp down there." He raised his voice toward the little dell below them. "Hello, the camp! I'm with the Forest Service. Anybody home?"

No answer.

"I don't like it." He unholstered his pistol. "You stay here while I check it out."

The camp had been concealed beneath camouflage canvas and dried brush. He could smell the wet ash from the doused camp fire. He searched overhead and spotted the plastic garbage bags suspended high in the pines. Whoever these guys were, they knew enough to protect their provisions from bears. They had struck their tent and stowed it under what could have passed for a deadfall. Another pile of brush covered a hole, which contained a nice cache of high-powered ammunition. These poachers were better supplied than any rebel squad Seth had "advised" in Central America. He left everything exactly as he'd found it and returned to the escarpment, where Mariah waited for him.

"I'll call this in when we get back," he told her. She nodded, and he thought her eyes held a hint of the regret he felt. The helicopter would be there in the morning. By noon she would be gone, and once these interlopers were caught, he would have his high country to himself again, at least until he shut the station down for winter. He would have the solitude he had spent the past years guarding. But something told him he'd be hard-pressed to reclaim the contentment being alone had once brought him.

Mariah glanced down at the nearly concealed camp. "I hope you catch these guys," she said.

"We'll catch them if they hang around another day. The way they botched that grizzly, and then all that ammo they've got down there..." Seth scowled and shook his head. "They must have gotten up here on horseback, and they probably have a four-wheel drive pickup and a trailer stashed somewhere. Poachers usually keep moving. My guess is they'll be long gone by to-morrow."

"What would you do if you didn't have me along? Would you wait for them?"

"Doesn't matter. I do have you along."

On the way back to the station they topped a rise and stopped to survey a shady basin and the scrub-covered slopes above it. The trickle of sliding rocks echoed in the pines below. Seth raised his binoculars and scanned the slope, top to bottom. He stopped, smiled, then offered Mariah a look. Slipping an arm around her shoulders, he pointed toward a distant stand of whitebark pine. "Griz-zlies," he said. "Mama and two cubs."

Mariah peered through the binoculars. It took a few seconds to locate the big brown bear, who was lumbering down the slope, followed by her bounding cubs. The afternoon's long shadows helped them to blend in with the sedge-covered mountainside. They were headed for a stream that was running high from yesterday's rainfall. The sow reached the water first, and the two babies piled into her rear like tumbling dominoes. Mariah laughed. At this distance, they could have been teddy bears rolling down a slide. She heard the click and whir of Seth's camera and wondered when he had dropped to one knee.

The mother bear suddenly sniffed the air and bolted for the trees. The babies jerked around as if she were towing them on a tandem leash. In her flight the sow seemed to take on a new shape, stretching her forelegs and covering ground with a grace and speed that belied her mass.

"Did she hear us?" Mariah asked.

"She smelled us." Seth unscrewed the zoom lens as he stood. "The wind shifted direction. Didn't you feel it?"

"I don't feel any wind."

"There's always some movement eddying down into the draws. It changes direction at the drop of a hat." He took the binoculars and shoved them into their case. "What did you think?"

Mariah's green eyes glistened with her broad smile. "Oh, Seth, you were right. It's nothing like seeing them in a zoo. Here they're so…"

"Free."

Chapter Five

Mariah poked through the shelves in the cabin's pantry looking for inspiration. Seth had decried the "domestic scene," and perhaps she had wanted to share some semblance of domesticity with him to make things *feel* right. Not that she believed she'd done anything really *wrong*. It was just that she needed to feel better about it—about him. She had an idea that good meals and good conversation might smooth everything over.

Except that—she reached for a can of boned chicken—she and Seth obviously had different ideas about what *smooth* meant. Still, she thought he liked her, whether he wanted to or not. If she went away with nothing but that, she would be content.

And tomorrow she would go away. He was calling in his report right now, maybe even mentioning her. They probably needed to know they'd have an extra passenger. She would be ready. She couldn't keep running. No, she *hadn't* been running, she told herself. A little retreat, that was all this was. Now it was up to her to deal with her father and get on with her life. She smiled as she stretched the fingers of her free hand around two more cans and remembered the little plaque she had seen in a gift shop recently. ''This is the first day of the rest of your life.'' As trite as it was, she'd made that promise to herself the day she'd set off on this journey. So maybe it would be tomorrow. The rest of her life had to start sometime.

''Mariah, come look. It's snowing.''

Seth was standing beside the open door and shaking the white flakes from his olive-green jacket. He carried a box under his arm, and the white sparkles in his hair were reproduced in his eyes as she emerged from the back room.

''Got some stuff I want to show you, but come look outside first,'' he invited. ''Too bad you didn't bring your skis.''

She smiled at the way he made it sound as though they had planned her visit, and what a shame it was they hadn't anticipated snow. She set the supper ingredients on the sideboard next to the stove and padded across the cabin floor on bare feet. ''Probably won't stick this first time, hmm?''

''It'll stick. It's coming down pretty good.'' He tossed his jacket over a chair. ''Better put something on your feet.''

''I left some water for you. I just took a quick shower.''

''All the more reason, if you're wet.'' He set the box on the bed and brought her a pair of his socks. ''There, put these on, and then come to the door.''

She sat on his jacket and pulled the socks over her feet. "Did you reach your headquarters?"

"Yeah. They're coming up tomorrow." He turned his back and shoved his hands into his pockets as he stared through the open door, into the night. "Told 'em they'd have a passenger. I didn't tell them your name. You can...make one up if you want to."

"I don't have any reason to," she assured him as she stepped up behind him.

He glanced down, then took her by the elbow. "It's a pretty night."

The snow sifted from a bright gray-white sky and settled over the ground like a confectioner's dusting. With only the kerosene glow behind them, it was the lack of man-made light that made the night so pretty. The snow was luminous. Its freshness made all things new. Seth stepped over the threshold, and when Mariah followed, he turned and scooped her up in his arms.

"Can't have you running around in the snow without shoes."

She laughed and put her arms around his neck.

"Look straight up," he ordered.

She did. It was dizzying. "Millions of parachutes."

"D day," he said. "They're coming to liberate you."

"I can liberate myself." She stuck out her tongue and caught several cold puffs on its tip. They burst into water. "All these little parachutes have to do is make me a path and I'll glide over them." She looked at Seth, nearly touching her nose to his. "Do you ski?"

"Not the way you do."

"Downhill?"

"I get to the bottom eventually. I was a flatlander growing up. Kind of got a late start on the sport."

"Have you ever tried cross-country?" He shook his

head. "Bet you'd be good at it. Perfect for a flatlander." She gave that image some thought. "I guess I thought you must have been born in these mountains."

The melting of a snowflake of her lower lip had caught his attention. He shook his head. "South Dakota." He wanted to taste that glistening bit of snowmelt. "Aberdeen."

"I've never been there. When did you leave?"

"When I was eighteen." He tore his thoughts away from the temptation to taste her lips, but he found just as much attraction in her soft eyes. "Getting cold?" he asked.

Cold? She smiled, trying to remember what cold was. "Getting hungry?" she wondered.

He hadn't thought about food in a while, but hungry? "You might say that."

"I haven't even started supper. Put me down, and I promise to make it quick."

Seth didn't move. He stood there watching the snow gather in the dark hair that swept across her forehead. She blinked when a flake fell on her eyelash, and he smiled and shifted her in his arms.

"Am I getting heavy?"

"No."

It was so quiet they could almost hear each snowflake as it landed.

"It *is* a pretty night," Mariah said.

"We've established that."

And what else? she wondered as she sought answers in the depths of his dark eyes. Have we established some inkling of trust? His misty breath kissed her cheek, but she wished for his lips and some whispered word of assurance. They were close, so breathlessly close that the wondering and the doubt became painful.

"Let's go inside," she suggested. As Seth turned toward the cabin she added impulsively, "After supper we can turn out the lamp and watch the night through the window."

He studied her for a moment. Seductress or innocent? Which was she? After supper, if reason didn't fail him, he would retreat to the lookout tower. On the other hand, hell, she'd be leaving tomorrow. Maybe he should forget the gallantry. She didn't seem to expect it.

He set her down just inside the door. "What are you planning?"

"Chicken pot pie," she said, her voice bright with promise. "I think I can do quite a nice one in the Dutch oven."

Innocent or seductress? he wondered again as he busied himself with fire building, his favorite distraction.

Mariah's chicken pot pie struck Seth as another culinary miracle performed from unlikely elements. His palate was accustomed to his own bland concoctions, and his stomach had adjusted to food that was ill prepared because he had little interest in cooking for himself and less in eating, so it was generally cold. His mind might have rejected the "domestic scene," but his digestive system found comfort in Mariah's cooking, and he decided to enjoy it while he could.

While the food didn't seem to impress Mariah much, the opportunity for conversation apparently did. Seth listened to her talk about teaching children how to read, about dealing with tattletales and bullies, about the time it took to get a class bundled up for recess in winter and peel off the wet wraps ten minutes later. She became more animated with each story, and he was captivated by the spark in her eyes.

"You don't get this excited when you talk about making the U.S. Ski Team," he observed. "That's a pretty big deal, too, isn't it?"

"It's a very big deal." Her tone didn't quite match the words. "A patriotic commitment, I'm told. Believe me, I don't take it lightly at all."

"I believe you. You must have been training pretty hard all summer. I can see why you'd need to take a break."

"Just to get my thoughts together. Priorities straight, as my father says." She looked at him as though she needed to convince him of something. "But, you see, they're *my* priorities. I have to do what's right for *me*."

"And that kind of competition isn't," he surmised, watching her carefully.

"Not now."

She wasn't well. He knew that if he asked her, she would tell him about it, and he didn't want to hear it. Illness was a private matter. Don't pry, he warned himself. He knew he'd get tangled up in his sympathy and her fear, and he told himself he didn't want any of that. He hadn't wanted what she had given him the previous night—the care, the *caring*—but she'd persisted. So, okay, he'd soaked it up like a sponge. That was his first mistake. Maybe his second. Three strikes and he could well be out of something called control, which he valued highly.

"Then maybe you oughta tell them all that," he suggested, although it was against his better judgment to make any suggestions. "Whoever's involved."

"Mostly my father and my coach," she said. She poked at her food. "I have, but they don't want to hear me. They say we've come too far."

Seth's fingers tightened around his fork. Too far? Couldn't they see how little she was eating, and how tired she got when— Back off, he told himself. He managed a casual shrug. "Sounds like you've gotta decide whether to fish or cut bait."

"Which is more like fishing?" She looked up at him intensely, as though she thought he might really know the answer when she wasn't even posing the whole question. "Is it skiing or...or something as mundane as teaching?"

"I guess it depends on who's writing your definitions, Mariah." He dropped the fork on his plate, letting it clatter like a solid piece of punctuation. "Is there any more of this stuff?"

"Yes, plenty."

She reached for his plate, but he shoved his chair back quickly. "I'll get it. Can I warm that up for you?"

"No, I'm fine."

Fine, hell. He had to bite his tongue to keep his doubts to himself.

"Do you have a family in South Dakota?" she asked quietly.

"My parents are still on the farm, but my brother's running it. I've got a sister who lives in Huron, South Dakota, and one in Sioux Falls."

"Do you get back there often?"

"No."

"Not even for holidays or—"

"I'm usually at least two months behind on the calendar," he quipped impatiently. "They know I'm alive, and I know where they are, so I figure we're not out of touch."

He kept his back to her as he recalled his mother's cast-iron skillet with the glass lid much like the one he was removing from the Dutch oven. He remembered the little blue pictures of pots and pans on the wallpaper in the kitchen. He'd once helped himself to good hot food from that skillet, too.

He had tried going home after the war, but it hadn't worked. They hadn't quite known what to make of him, and he hadn't known how to tell them where he'd been and what he'd seen. What he'd done. Everybody said how nice it was that he'd won all those medals, and they were proud of the way he'd done his duty, but now it was all over and best forgotten, especially since he and his fellow soldiers hadn't exactly come home in triumph.

Years later, only his father had come to see him in the VA hospital. The visit had marked a turning point in Seth's treatment. At the sight of his reserved, remote father, his fragile shell had exploded in the old man's face, a loss of control that still gave him a sick feeling in the pit of his stomach when he thought about it. Cursing, raving, spitting with every word, he had confessed his self-hatred to the one person left in his life who would at least listen.

John Cantrell had listened, but he had not understood. "You came through the war just fine, son. Just a few scratches. Don't know why you had to hire out to them South Americans and get that damned malaria."

"Malaria?" The word had drawn Seth down a long, dark tunnel and squeezed a reaction from him. No one knew him. Not even the man who had raised him. "Look at me, old man," he had pleaded. "Can't you see I'm so screwed up I can't see straight? Can't you see what I've done?"

There had been a sad shaking of his father's sun-withered, gray head, and Seth had thought that his father was refusing to see him.

"They tell me it's from mosquitoes."

The old man's glasses were fogged. He *couldn't* see.

"It's blood, Dad, not mosquitoes. Women's blood. Children's. Armless, legless, headless men…Dad!"

"You were always a good boy, son." The head kept shaking. The man saw the boy he'd once known, not the terrible man the boy had become. "Some things in life can't be helped."

What couldn't be helped? It was a question Seth still hadn't answered for himself. He took his plate back to the table and avoided Mariah's eyes while he ate. She didn't know him, either, and that was fine. Carnal knowledge was all he ever intended that she should have of him. Good sex was the best he could offer her—or any woman, for that matter. Not even Carla had ever faulted him in bed.

Mariah finished the last of the biscuit crust on her plate. She was still smarting from the way Seth had cut off their conversation. He'd revealed more of himself the previous night, when he'd been half out of his mind with fever, than he had since she'd known him. But now that they were sitting across from each other at the table again, obviously his family was off-limits. She laid her fork down, and suddenly her plate was snatched from under her nose. She frowned as she watched him pile it on top of his.

"I promised to show you some pictures," he said, determined to shake off the oppressive dust of the past.

"You did?"

"Well, yeah, I told you I had—" he jerked his head in the direction of the bed, and she remembered the box "—something to show you." He smiled as he pushed his chair back and lifted the plates. The room seemed to brighten with the change in his mood. "More bighorns," he offered as he dumped the tin plates in the dishpan. "More bears, goats, elk, eagles. What do you like best?"

"Squirrels." She returned with a smile.

"Squirrels?"

"When I'm skiing, I love it when they dart out in front of me, like we're racing."

"Squirrels." He shrugged. "I guess I've got a few— hey, I've got a great shot of a flying squirrel. You know, they're hard to photograph. You just don't see them, and when you do, you blink, and it's too late."

They sat together on the bed, with the kerosene lantern on the table close by. The hinges on the big metal box squeaked as Seth tipped the lid back. He took out a handful of glossy five-by-seven color photographs and handed her the first one. "You like squirrels? This little freeloader ruined my lunch."

Mariah grinned at the picture, which was the kind that was worth a thousand words. A ground squirrel had popped its head up from the pocket of a bright orange backpack to have its picture taken. Seth handed her another shot of the squirrel scampering over the top of the pack with a piece of hardtack in its mouth.

"You shouldn't leave your pack on the ground like that," she chided with a laugh.

"You should if you want a terrific picture. Look at the wildflowers—the blue lupines and the white mountain meadowsweet next to that orange pack. Nice colors, huh?"

"Beautiful." Mariah admired them even as he pushed another picture into her hand.

"I used a 300mm lens to get this coyote. I like the long, gray shadow on the snow. God, he was pretty. You should have heard him howl. Okay—" He slipped her another picture. She glanced up and saw a mature version of the expression that had accompanied many a crayon drawing presented for her approval. Excitement. Expectation. Pride. "Here's your flying squirrel."

"My flying squirrel?"

"*My* flying squirrel," he corrected. "They bought this shot for a children's wildlife magazine."

"Which magazine?"

"*Animals All Around Us.* I think that's what they call it."

Mariah nodded, enjoying the certainty that he knew darn well what they called it. "I've seen that. It's a good magazine. We have it in our school library. I'll have to look for this iss—"

"Here's an elk," he declared as he slid another photograph on top of the one she held. "It was that time before dawn when the air gets still, kind of waiting. The light was just right to give it that blue cast."

"He looks big."

Seth moved closer and pointed to the corner of the picture. "You can get an idea of his size if you compare him to this—" her hair held the scent of the pine woods, and the neckline of her flannel shirt arrowed past a hint of the curve of her breast "—rock. Fairly large…rock."

Mariah turned to discover the bright heat in his eyes. "These are wonderful. You…free-lance, then?"

"Some. My job is seasonal."

If eyes could devour, she would have been swallowed up by his.

"But not your photography."

"No. I'm always taking—" He tunneled his fingers into her thick hair. "Always taking pictures. Never… your hair reminds me of something wild."

"I know." She swallowed convulsively. "I can't seem to tame it."

"Don't try." He let it slide slowly between his fingers. "It's beautiful. It's natural. I thought I would—"

His kiss came as no surprise. Mariah saw it coming and knew what shock waves it would send crashing through her. She had felt them before—that night. *That night.* Shamelessly, selfishly, she wanted that night again. She felt a tug on the pictures, and she relaxed her hands and let him take them away. She put her arms around him and flattened her palms against his back, feeling his strength beneath the thick ribbing of his cotton sweater. He moved his mouth over hers, paying genuine lip service to each curve and contour as he guided her toward the center of the bed and gave her a place to lay her head. He moved his body over hers.

"I thought I could get through this night without—" Her face needed to be kissed. Her temple, cheek, chin— every inch demanded attention. "But, God, you're beautiful."

"So are you," she whispered. "I thought so from the first."

"First time you saw me?" He nuzzled her neck.

"First time you held me." She closed her eyes and relished the shiver that shimmied like a quick ripple of water from her neck to her toes.

There was a difference, but it would probably take a woman to explain it right. He didn't want to get into that. He nudged at the vee of her shirtfront and told himself that *this* was all he wanted to get into.

"If I just kiss you…"

"Yes, that's all," she whispered. "Just hold me and kiss me." She felt her buttons give in to him, too, one by one. His hand was sure and unerring. The plastic fastener of her bra gave way without a test. She took a deep breath, and her breasts were unbound.

She was ready before he even touched her, he thought, but touch her he did. He teased her with the tip of his nose, and then his lips came nibbling. Her breasts were smooth and round and easy, so easy on the skin. Too easy. Too damn easy. But then came the hard part, small and round and made for suckling, and he did it for her, because he wanted to make her tingle. He wanted to make her heart beat faster and her insides hurt the way his did. So she wouldn't make it so easy—damn it—so easy to suck on her like some mewling baby who was so hungry he couldn't help himself.

Mariah threaded her fingers into his hair and held him to her breast because, yes! he was going to give her that night again, but not as a stranger this time. This time she would be Mariah, and he would be loving Mariah and no one else. She was melting inside. He held her hips and laved her breasts with the tip of his tongue while he rocked himself against the insides of her thighs. Soon he would call her name and let her know...

"Damn, I oughta know better," he mumbled as he reached for the snap on her jeans. "But I can't help remembering...can't help wanting..."

"It's all right, Seth." *Say my name, please.* "Some things can't be—"

"Can't be helped?" He groaned. *Some things can't be helped.* Damn. He pushed himself up suddenly, dragging his hips against her just to punish himself. "You're right."

Bracing himself on one elbow, he bent the opposite knee, giving himself some space as he snatched her hand and pushed it against him. "I can't help this. Watching you, smelling you, touching you—this is how I get." She stared up at him, wide-eyed, her breasts quivering with each chest-heaving breath. She excited him. He sickened himself. "Is it like this with you?" he persisted.

"Seth, don't—"

"Don't what?" He let her go, but even as she drew her hand back, he passed his between her legs. "Don't stop? This is what you came for, isn't it? You've got the same thing going on with you that's going on with me, right?"

"I guess…I guess I…"

"Uh-uh, no games. No guesses. The first time you *saw* me, you liked what you saw. Simple as that."

"Why are you doing this?"

"Because last night I was—" He shook his head and slid his hand over her stomach. She closed her eyes, and he had to steel himself against a niggling stab of regret. His voice softened. "I just want to get one thing straight, Mariah. I don't need to be held. Don't kid yourself. The only thing I need from any woman is a good, quick—"

A tear slipped from the corner of her eye, glinting in the lamplight as it raced to hide itself in her hair. Her shoulders trembled. Her breasts—once freely given, now simply exposed—quivered as a second tear chased the first one.

Seth clenched his teeth and waited for that old numbness to spare him from guilt. It wouldn't come. He eased himself off her, grabbed his jacket and left without a word.

Mariah pulled her shirt together. The need for him still throbbed deep inside her, and she sat up quickly to douse the lantern, as if she were afraid someone might witness her humiliation. She gave in to her tears because she wanted to be rid of them, and when they were spent, she went to the back room and washed her face. She told herself it wasn't the first mistake she'd ever made and probably wouldn't be the last. Not sure what had happened, she decided it had to be his problem, not hers. She wasn't trying to trap him. She was only trying to…

What was she trying to do? Learn about him? Become his friend? Make more of this than there actually was? She felt foolish. She'd made an offer, and he'd found it quite resistible. With a horrible, hollow feeling in the pit of her stomach, she crawled into his bed. She stared at the beamed ceiling. Sleep wouldn't come. She thought of all the things she might say to him tomorrow, and all the ways she might word them. None of them worked, not even in her mind.

The knock on the door brought her bolt upright. The door opened slowly, and Seth stepped inside. He stood there briefly, and when she said nothing, he went to her, expecting her to curse him at any moment. She didn't.

He stopped at the foot of the bed, looking awkward, because he wanted to move closer but didn't quite dare. "Look, I'm sorry." The words sounded pitifully inadequate to his own ears, but he pressed on. "What I said a while ago, the way I…it was all wrong."

Mariah clutched the blankets on either side of her hips and held her breath. When she didn't send him away, he took a step closer, then another, and finally sat next to her on the bed. She watched his every move, but still said nothing.

"It's been a very long time since I've…since I've even been with the same woman more than once." He chuckled softly in self-derision. "For obvious reasons. Things start to get complicated, and I'm—" enough light came through the window to allow her to see the outline of his profile and he shook his head "—just no good at it."

He wished she would say something to make this a little easier, but she just sat there, ramrod stiff and clutching those blankets. As if she were scared of him. The notion struck him like a blow in his gut, leaving him just sitting there, too.

"I wouldn't hurt you," he said quietly. "I didn't come in here to try to—"

"I know." Her voice was a small echo of itself.

"I made it sound like I thought you wanted to get—"

"Don't, Seth."

"I knew better," he said as he lifted his hand toward her tentatively. She sat very still, waiting. He touched her cheek, and she pressed it against his palm, giving him the tears he'd tried to run from earlier. "Mariah, I'm sorry." He groaned as he pulled her into his arms.

She buried her face against his neck, which felt cool and smelled like a winter's night, and she let him hold her while she stemmed her streaming tears. "But you were right," she confessed at last. "I did want you."

"Not the way I made it sound."

"What difference does it make?"

"Careful," he warned, and he pushed her hair back from her forehead and kissed her there. "You say stuff like that too often, you might start believing it."

"Don't you?"

"I thought I did." He eased her head into the protective hollow beneath his chin and stroked her hair. "After I left I felt like something that should've been slithering into a hole."

She closed her eyes, savoring the comfort he offered. It wasn't fair to let him take all the blame. "I've been a nuisance for you. I never should have come here."

His hand stilled in her hair. "Why *did* you come, Mariah?"

What should she tell him? What would he accept from her now? The truth, she told herself. At least a part of it.

"Because I wanted to see you again."

If you ask her why, she'll tell you, a little voice whispered in his head. This woman gives more than she gets, and you've taken enough already.

He swallowed hard. "It feels good to hold you again."

She felt like a passenger whose plane had just taken flight.

"And you'll be leaving tomorrow," he said quietly.

"I know."

"Let me stay," he whispered. "Let me hold you tonight."

As soon as she said yes, he took off his jacket, his boots and his shirt, and she moved over and flipped the corner of the covers aside. He went to her and held her the way he knew she wanted him to, kissed her and promised himself that this time he would discover what pleased her and give her the best of what little he had to offer.

But she turned the tables on him. He unbuttoned her shirt and touched her breasts, kissed them, molded her nipples into hard, tight little tips, but he was harder. His pants felt tight. Uncomfortably so. Somehow she knew, and she slipped her hand between them and unsnapped, unzipped. Her fingertips grazed him as he sprang free. He sucked his breath in sharply, and she responded to the sound with a benevolent caress, filling him with sweet bliss. He let it build until it was close to the point of pain, and then he remembered his vow. He snatched her hand away and slanted his lips over hers, thrusting his tongue into her mouth while his hand went in search of the means to bring her to the same dizzying urgency.

She told herself it would be different this time.

He told himself it would be better this time.

Their estimates fell short of what would be.

He found a damp nest, and he let his fingers play back and forth along the edge. She sighed, and her stomach fluttered against the heel of his hand.

What did she want from him?

What would he allow her to give him?

What would it take to make this right for her?

It took only the touch of his hand. He knew just how to bring her to the brink, back off and bring her there again. When he felt her trembling in his hand like a small bird, trapped and begging to be released, he slipped inside her and gave her leave to fly away.

The instant she soared, he joined her, and when she returned, she returned to him. Through the night, they held each other just because it felt right.

By morning it had stopped snowing. The fir trees and the mountain slopes were blanketed in soft white, and the cabin felt like a snug cocoon. Seth kissed Mariah awake, and he decided her sleepy, satisfied smile was better than strong coffee for getting his heart pumping in the morning.

"Sleep well?" he asked as he hovered over her.

"Hmm."

"Hungry?"

"For what?"

He chuckled. "Anything. You name it."

"Corn flakes and huckleberries with—"

"You'd send me out after huckleberries?"

"Fresh milk."

He groaned and rolled over onto his back. "I've gotta find a cow, too?"

"You said *anything.*"

"Guess I'd better get started." He flipped the blankets back, leaving his body beautifully exposed. "Be back around nightfall."

Mariah slipped her arms around Seth's waist and pressed her cheek against his shoulder. "I can make do with just corn flakes."

"No milk?"

"No milk. Do you mind if we get crumbs in the bed?"

"You talking about me, woman?" He hooked his arm around her shoulder and snuggled back down while she covered him up again. "I came crawling back last night just so you wouldn't go off thinking I was such a crumb."

"I have no objection to crumbs in the bed," she protested sweetly. "Obviously."

"Obviously," he mimicked, and he dipped his head to nip her shoulder. Suddenly he stiffened, then stretched his neck like a buck who'd caught scent of something dangerous.

"What's wrong?"

"Shh." His arms tightened around her as he listened. She heard nothing. Not even a bird. "Chopper," he announced finally as he threw back the covers and rolled over on one hip. "Get dressed, quick. What the hell are they doing up this early?" He grabbed his jeans off the floor and tossed the flannel shirt she'd worn to bed over his shoulder.

Mariah stared numbly at the ripple of blue plaid that had landed on her belly. Not yet, she thought. We haven't...

"Get some clothes on, honey." Seth disappeared into the back room. "They'll be banging on that door before you know it."

Her mind was moving faster than her fingers could manage. The buttons on her shirt wouldn't cooperate. She could hear the staccato chug of the rotor for herself now as the helicopter drew closer.

"Straighten out that bed," came the order from the back room. "Damn, I hate that sound. I'll get the stove going so it just looks like we're having breakfast." He stuck his head out the door, and she hopped up from the bed as though she'd been caught red-handed. He was already dressed. "So it looks like we're doing something other than what we're—honey, I'm not kidding. That thing's about to drop in our—"

"I can't go yet." She hurried across the room, nearly tripping over a chair along the way.

"I know." Seth dropped his hand from the door frame and caught her when she came to him. She'd gotten a button wrong, and he quickly undid the top two so he could fix it for her. "This was kind of a rude awakening, but we don't have any control over the taxi service here, and I don't want anybody walking in and—"

"We have to talk, Seth."

He studied her for a second, the chopper blades whirring in his ears. "How about…if I got to Bozeman sometime. I wouldn't interfere with your ski season, but maybe next spring—"

"Not next spring," she said desperately.

"Whenever. Would you—" Seth jerked his head toward the window. The helicopter had touched down on the flat next to the lookout tower. He reversed their positions, pushing her back into the pantry. "You have to get dressed."

"Don't tell them I'm here," she pleaded.

His eyes hardened as he gripped her shoulders tighter. "Why not?"

"I'm pregnant, Seth. That's what I came to tell you." She sagged a little in his hands. "I just thought you…I thought you should know."

He stared at her for a moment as though he were seeing her for the first time. Then he abruptly set her away from him, turned on his heel and left the cabin.

Chapter Six

The helicopter's blades created a localized snow squall in the small mountain meadow above the cabin. Seth's thoughts whirled the same way, his anger kicking up a cloud of confusion as he negotiated the rocky path from the cabin to the tower. He had half a mind to put Mariah Crawford on that chopper along with all her schemes and send her packing without further discussion.

Half a mind. That was about all he had left for the job he was supposed to be doing up here. He stopped several yards from the helicopter, shoved his hands into his jacket pockets and waited. Howard Polanski alighted, ducking the spinning blades as he held on to the earflaps of his Cossack-style cap with both hands. The wind caught his open jacket, and his game warden's shield glinted on his shirt pocket.

"So where's our passenger?" Polanski shouted, glancing up at the tower windows. Polanski had a habit of asking a question, then peering behind a person as if the *real* answer might be there to be found.

Seth envisioned Polanski discovering Mariah, and he shook his head. "No passenger. Just some crazy poacher on the loose."

"Dispatcher plainly said *passenger*," Polanski bawled in Seth's face. Seth wasn't sure which was more annoying—the blast of wind from the chopper or Polanski's manner. "He thought you'd come across some overzealous climber or something."

"Must have misunderstood. I said I had a poacher."

"Well, he told us about that, too. We got another one upriver on the Flathead we gotta check out."

"'Tis the season." Seth indicated the helicopter with a jerk of his chin. "Take me up. I'll show you where he was camped."

Pilot Charlie Day gave Seth a jovial shoulder punch as he crawled into the passenger's seat. Charlie was okay. He kept his ears under the headset, and he wasn't always asking Seth how he tolerated all this isolation or hinting for the details of his activities after he'd taken a couple of days off. Charlie wasn't nosy. Seth could have put Mariah in the seat beside Charlie, and Charlie would have flown her back to civilization, no questions asked. But not Polanski.

Seth navigated for Charlie, and they found a spot to set the aircraft down near the campsite so that Seth and Polanski could investigate. It was no surprise when they found only a caved-in hole and a buried fire pit, all nicely covered with a three-inch blanket of snow.

Polanski nosed around a while before confronting Seth, shifting his weight from one leg to the other and back again while he chose his words. Seth Cantrell wasn't

someone Polanski wanted to offend. Seth waited, antici-
pating the obvious question.

"After you located this spot, why didn't you hang
around 'til these trigger-happy yahoos came back?"

Seth conceded to himself that the question was not
only obvious, it was reasonable, and he almost regretted
having to come up with a lie for an answer. "I was unarmed."

"You? Unarmed?"

Seth stared. *Take it or leave it.*

"But you'd just had a wounded bear up here the other
day. You mean to tell me you were walkin' around
here—"

"With a camera. I was out taking pictures."

Polanski raised a finger to make a point, but the look
in Seth's eyes made him lower it again. "Y'oughta carry
a side arm at least, Cantrell. You never know."

"I'll keep that in mind, Polanski."

"Well, no point in crying over spilled milk. This guy's
probably up in Glacier by now."

"Probably."

They headed back up the hill toward the helicopter.
"You anxious to shut down for the winter, Cantrell?"

"Not especially. I'd like to see this poacher stopped."

"Yeah, well, there's a lot of nothing up here. A guy
can make himself pretty hard to find," Polanski com-
mented as they trudged through the knee-high brush.
"Charlie brought supplies. I guess you can look forward
to a few more weeks. Don't know how you mountain
men stay sane." He chuckled. "When you hit town, bet
you've got just one thing on your mind, and anything
that's female better look out."

Seth clenched his teeth as his soles crunched in the
snow. There was no way Polanski was getting near the

cabin, and no way Mariah was getting in that chopper with him. Prying was this man's favorite pastime. His resentment over Mariah's schemes had momentarily slipped Seth's mind.

"C'mon, Polanski. I'll show you the grizzly carcass. Maybe you want a rug."

Mariah listened for the returning helicopter. When it came it was neither a welcome nor a dreaded sound. It was simply like a chime or a buzzer, announcing that it was time to take the next step. The only thing was, she wasn't sure what was going on, so she hadn't decided what the next step would be. Like the skilled athlete that she was, she tried to anticipate. It seemed logical that the poacher must have been first on the rangers' agenda, but the crazy woman who had climbed far too high was bound to be next. She had dressed and packed. She would take the next step just as she had taken each of the others since she'd confirmed her pregnancy. One at a time.

World-class athletes did not get pregnant, according to Edward Crawford's dictum.

But women sometimes did, his daughter pointed out.

Careless, but correctable. A woman who was preparing for the Olympic trials would do the sensible thing. She would abort the pregnancy.

Mariah had considered that option and rejected it, but her father had refused to accept her decision. She had listened to him until she could no longer stand to hear the listing of expenditures—money, time, hopes, dreams, commitments. Under the incessant verbal barrage she felt guilty. She doubted herself. She was not so much afraid of her father as of her own inability to think for herself whenever he was around. Finally she left her father a message specifying nothing but that she would return within the week, and she slipped away.

Stealing some time for herself had been crucial while she contemplated another problem. Where did the father of her baby fit in? Telling him seemed the decent thing to do. She'd come a long way to do just that, and then he hadn't even recognized her at first. She had anticipated almost any reaction but that one. She'd felt insignificant and dislocated. Perhaps the night she remembered hadn't really happened, at least not the way *she* remembered it.

But she *was* pregnant, and Seth Cantrell was the father of her baby. She knew little more about him now than she had before, but that little might be precious one day when his child would undoubtedly ask about him. And now, for better or for worse, she had shared more with him than just one fleeting, impulsive encounter. No matter what he thought of the news she'd brought him, Mariah would not regret this time she'd spent in the mountains.

The helicopter landed, and she waited, for she could see nothing from the cabin's windows but white peaks and blue-green treetops. She instructed herself in the art of feeling nothing. He'd said he would look her up next spring. If he did, fine. If he didn't, that would be fine, too. She had not come to make any demands. She had just thought he should know about the baby. That was all. He had a right to know. She had done the *right* thing. She had another step ahead of her, and then another, now that this one had been accomplished.

It surprised her when she heard the helicopter lift off again. She glanced at her backpack sitting beside the door and studied her gloved hands. They'd left without her. Then Seth passed by the window with his arms full of boxes, and the art of feeling nothing fell by the wayside.

His "Hey, Mariah, could you get the door?" sounded like an anthem.

Don't get into it right away, Seth warned himself as he waited. Just go on about your business. Don't ask a bunch of questions. The answers are bound to be full of complications.

The door swung open, and there she stood, all dressed for an outing. He saw the backpack, with her bedroll strapped to the bottom. She reached out to relieve him of part of his burden, and something inside his chest tightened. He had done what she'd asked him to do, but she was prepared to leave anyway.

"It's okay. I've got this," he assured her as he stepped inside, ignoring her offer to help.

"Is there more?"

"I'll get that, too."

She tried for a light tone and almost achieved it. "Does this mean you're not kicking me out?"

He walked past her, leaving her question to float for a while as he headed for the back room. The boxes landed in the center of the floor with a thud. Seth took refuge in the role of the man who had work to do, as he retraced his steps toward the door. But he couldn't pull off the effect of complete stoicism.

"What kind of a jerk would kick a pregnant woman out in this kind of weather?" he quipped just before he shut the door behind him.

Mariah took off her gloves and jacket and set to work unpacking the supplies. Seth soon returned with the last of them, and his first inclination was to tell her to back off and let him take care of it. She turned to him, clutching cans of peaches and mixed vegetables close to her chest, and gave him that wide-eyed, expectant look of hers. Expectant, for God's sake. He bit off his objections and snatched up a log to add to the fire, whether it was needed or not.

"Shall I fix us some breakfast?" she asked after she'd finished her job. She stood near the gas stove, where she felt most comfortable. With one hand braced against the stone mantel, he kept a brooding watch on the fire. He wasn't going to ask any questions. Not a one.

"I'm not hungry." He was, actually. He just didn't feel like eating.

Mariah moved closer and stationed herself near the heavy wooden table this time. "I guess we should talk."

Seth lifted his gaze slowly. "That's why you said you wanted to stay," he reminded her. "To talk."

"I know that was kind of a bad way to drop the news," she admitted as she gripped the back of a chair.

He shrugged and turned his attention back to the flicker in the fireplace. "Good a way as any, I guess. It's the next part you've gotta be careful with."

"The next part?"

"You're gonna try to tell me this is my kid."

She rolled her hands back and forth around the top of the hand-hewn ladder-back chair and told herself to stay calm. "It is."

The fire seemed as agitated as he was inside. The flames shuddered and darted, seemingly frustrated with their containment. "It doesn't happen like this," he muttered. "If there's a God in heaven, it's not allowed to happen like this." The look he gave her was almost plaintive. "Why me?"

"What do you mean, why you?"

"What makes you think it was me?"

Her stomach began churning slowly. "Look, I'm sorry I bothered you with it. I just thought you should know because—"

She eyed him carefully as she took her hands away from the chair. She didn't need its support as her indignation mounted. "What makes me *think* it was you?" She stepped around the table like a stalking house cat. "I may have spent a good part of my life with my head in the clouds, Seth Cantrell, but I do know how babies are made. Maybe I didn't know much about you, but at least *I* recognized *you* immediately when I saw you again, and you were the only man—"

"The only man *that night*, maybe."

The sound of the slap surprised her, and it surprised her even more to see the pink imprint of her smarting hand on his cheek. He hadn't expected it, either, and he grabbed her wrist only after the damage was done.

"The only one," she repeated, carefully measuring each syllable.

"Now you're going to explain to me how I'm too callous to know when I've got a virgin on my hands."

"No, I'm not." She jerked her wrist, and he released her. "I've told you all I came to tell you."

"As I recall, I asked you whether you were prepared, and you said you were."

She tried to remember the question, the answer, or any kind of caution playing a part in her actions that night, but all she could recall was a wonderful need and a determination to fulfill it. In retrospect, the feeling seemed foolish. The wind shifted, and her sails drooped.

Seth's filled. "What's the matter? Your memory failing you all of a sudden? Honey, you were so ready and so willing, it didn't surprise me at all when you said you were prepared."

"I thought you meant—" She was embarrassed now to realize what she'd thought he meant. *Are you prepared for this?* This what? Her imagination had supplied lovely answers. This moment. This experience. This gift. What a fool she'd been.

He watched her lower herself to the settee, and it was as though she were sinking, shrinking, sliding away from him. *She* had just hit *him*, for God's sake, but he felt as though he'd been the one to land the blow. Before he knew it, he was sitting next to her.

"You thought I meant what?"

"Nothing." She turned her attention quickly to the fire. "I don't know what I thought. Obviously, I wasn't thinking clearly that night."

"I guess I should have seen that."

She shook her head quickly. "I'm not blaming you."

"But you're sure…?"

She nodded without taking her eyes off the fire. "You're the father."

"I mean, there's no doubt you're…"

"No doubt." She hugged her knees and studied the red stone in her college ring. "I thought a lot about telling you—how to say it, what your response might be. I didn't expect you to be overjoyed, but I guess I never imagined you'd doubt that it was yours."

"Mariah…" He sighed. She'd put that ski cap on again, and now her hair was full of static electricity. He lifted his forefinger, unsure whether he should touch her, but that wonderfully wild hair didn't hesitate to stand up and greet him. He remembered the way it swung around her face when she danced.

"You were standing there alone that night, and you looked so damn good. There was rain all around us and music in the distance, and when I held you and kissed you, you didn't—"

She closed her eyes, as if doing so might bring back the best part. "It felt so good when you held me."

"Damn, what...how could you be so—"

Her green eyes suddenly challenged him again. "So stupid?"

Quickly he lowered his hand to the back of the settee. "No. I just thought—"

"You thought I was there to get picked up? Is that what you thought?"

"You didn't try to stop me, Mariah."

"I didn't want to."

"Did you...intend to get pregnant?" She shook her head, and he gazed over the top of it, contemplating. "One lousy night. Less than one night. That's all we spent together."

"It doesn't...take a whole lot of time, does it?"

"No, I guess it doesn't."

She looked up at him. "I didn't think it was such a...such a lousy night."

"I didn't mean that." He moved his hand over her shoulder and squeezed. She looked slight, but there was strength beneath the flannel shirt. "I didn't mean it like that at all. I just meant...why didn't you tell me right away? As soon as you got here?"

"Because you didn't even know who I was."

He acknowledged his mistake with a lift of his brow. "You looked a lot different. I mean—"

"And when you figured it out, you thought I'd come here looking for—"

He groaned, remembering. "For more of the same thing that got you into this mess. And then last night..."

"Don't." She put her hand on his thigh and found the denim warm from the heat of the fire. "Don't say anything about last night. Just...let it be. Okay?"

"Okay." She was right. He didn't want to put last night through the wringer, either. "But I don't understand what you were doing with me that first night, Mariah. I wanted sex. I thought you did, too.''

She drew her hand back quickly. ''What if I did? Don't I have a right to want sex, too?''

''Sure, but—''

''Did I have to have another motive, just because I let myself be—'' she waved her hand, groping for the word ''—human, for once? Because I needed something besides protein or B vitamins or weight training? You were...'' She knew it was a mistake to try to tell him what she'd seen in him that night. He was looking for the sense of what she had done, and it didn't make any sense.

She rested her head against the log frame of the settee and closed her eyes. ''I don't know why, Seth. I just let myself go that night. I really don't understand why I did what I did.''

He kneaded her shoulder gently. ''What do you want me to do?''

''You don't have to do anything,'' she assured him as she lifted her head again. She was determined to hold her head up through this, and she hadn't been doing the best job of it. ''I just had this silly, probably very old-fashioned notion that it was right to tell you about it, that's all.''

''You want me to...marry you?''

''No.'' She managed to laugh, but it sounded shaky. ''I'm not *that* old-fashioned. I came to you because—'' She looked at him earnestly. The fire crackled nearby, and his hand soothed her. ''Because this is between us, and I thought we could talk about it. Really talk.''

''We probably should have talked about it before we, uh, before we did it.'' Damn, I asked you, Mariah. You said you were prepared.

"We hardly talked at all."

"That's right. Which means…" He waited for those eyes to flash at him again, and when they did, he found himself smiling. *Prepared* had been way out of reach that night. "You had a lot of nerve trekking all the way up here to see some guy you really knew nothing about—"

"Except that he's the father of my baby."

"Yeah." His smile faded. "Except that."

"And that he held me after we made love."

He remembered. It was not his custom to linger afterward, but he remembered that it had felt, just briefly, as if she belonged there in his arms. For a few moments he had been able to forget that they were lying on the floor of a place where neither of them belonged.

"I wanted to know more, Seth. I need to know who my baby's father is. What he's like."

He swallowed hard and turned his face toward the fire. "You've got plans? About the baby, I mean."

"I've tried to make plans, but everyone around me thinks I'm crazy. *Everyone* around me," she repeated, shaking her head. "There aren't that many, but of course I've told my father and my coach. There's no question in their minds. They want me to have an abortion and get on with my life. Get on with my skiing."

He realized that he hadn't been prepared to hear the word *abortion*. First she said he was going to be a father; then she said he might not be. Abortion. It was her decision, of course. But it gave him a funny, squeamish kind of feeling to hear her say it after she'd said it was his baby.

"Is that what you want?" he asked quietly.

"It's all I've heard, ever since I first told them about it."

"If it's what you want, and if you need some kind of help—you know, financially—"

She wanted his help. She wanted him to tell her that her gut feeling about all this was legitimate, that it was okay to want to be a mother to this baby. If he could tell her that, it would help.

"Is that what you think I should do?"

Good Lord, what a question. "Hell, what do I know? What do *you* want to do?"

"I want to have the baby."

"And…they're telling you you're crazy." She nodded. She looked lost, and he knew the feeling. He'd been told how crazy he was by a woman who'd once said she loved him. Her father and her coach clearly had no idea what "crazy" was. "You're not," he assured her. "If you want to have the baby, I think…I think that's fine. If that's what you want, it's fine."

"I know how much they've put into my skiing, both of them. And I know how far we've come. I know how close we are. It's just that—" she pressed her hand against her belly "—this is more important now."

"*This* baby?"

"*My* baby." He saw the wistfulness in her eyes and knew it came from other places in her life. Other times, other faces. "I love children. I already love this one. No one seems to understand—this one's mine."

Her baby. Hadn't she told him a few minutes ago that it was his, too? "So you've decided."

"I know what I want." The innocent wistfulness suddenly gave way to wariness. She looked to Seth for more assurance. "Maybe I'm being selfish. Maybe I'm not thinking about anyone but me."

She'd sure as hell eliminated him from the picture in short order. But wasn't that the way he wanted it? Minimize the complications. He lifted one shoulder as casually as he could manage. "You're the one who's pregnant."

"Yes, but—"

"So you're the one who has to decide." He stood. Maybe the fire needed tending. He grabbed the poker and gave one log a push. Sparks rushed up the chimney.

"I can get somebody up here to take you back when you're ready," he offered while he poked needlessly at another ash-coated log. "Maybe you just need some time to think."

"And someone to—"

"Someone to get some food in you once in a while." He put the poker back and closed the fireplace door. "You don't eat enough for one person, never mind two."

"I get a little queasy over food sometimes."

He looked at her, concerned. "Because of the baby?" She nodded, and he turned away abruptly. More complications. The thought of her discomfort made him feel solicitous, as though he'd be grateful for the opportunity to wait on her if she would just say the word. And that impulse made *him* feel uncomfortable. This was *her* baby. She'd made that clear. It was none of his business whether she got enough to eat.

"So how about some corn flakes?" Cantrell, you're an idiot. "And maybe...I could probably find some huckleberries for you, too."

Over the next two days Seth and Mariah picked their way around the cabin as though the wrong step might cause one of them to fracture something fragile. Seth spent time searching for signs of more poaching, while Mariah kept a lookout from the tower. For the most part she looked out for Seth's return.

He had slept in the lookout tower both nights. After supper he had lingered only a few moments before he said good-night and left the cabin. Mariah hadn't questioned him about it, but after spending long hours in the tower herself during the day, she wondered how he fared at night. It made her feel lonely to see his neatly rolled bedding stashed in the corner next to the small stove. She imagined him unrolling it in the dark and huddling next to the tower's meager heater.

Like a lover bearing flowers, he had brought her huckleberries, and he'd admonished her to enjoy them while she could. With the hard freeze, they were dropping off the bushes and would soon be scarce. They'd joked about making wine from frozen huckleberries and imagined what "happy campers" they would be all winter with the stash they could produce. But the laughter had died when they looked at one another, shared the wistful spark of warmth in each other's eyes, then looked away. They didn't have all winter. They had a few days, and they didn't quite know how to manage that time.

Mariah paged through several of the wildlife magazines she had found stashed in a drawer or on a shelf. Seth had a number of published photographs to his credit. His pictures extolled wildness. He had a way with light and shadow that gave the images a dreamlike aura, a sense that wilderness existed apart from the real world. Indeed, she had felt she was dreaming as she'd watched the bighorns and, later, the grizzlies. When the animals had sensed their part in the human dream, they had vanished.

The sound of footsteps on the metal steps below caught Mariah by surprise. She circled the map table and reached the door just in time to greet Seth, who saw that he'd caught her off guard.

"Didn't even see me coming, did you?" he asked as he pulled his gloves off and headed for the stove. "Sleeping on the job might just get you fired."

"I was watching—sort of." She reached furtively for the binoculars as she trailed him past the desk, brightly quipping, "All's quiet on the western front. Where there's no smoke, there's no fire, right?"

He looked up from the business of warming his hands and smiled. "You have a way with words. Can I quote you in the log?"

"Be my guest."

"So, what's it like on the eastern front?"

She shrugged. "Quiet there, too. I thought you'd be out all day. It's only noon."

"I was in the neighborhood. Thought I'd come back for lunch." He'd worked his way around to being "in the neighborhood" at lunchtime without making a conscious effort, but he knew what he'd done. Home for lunch, he thought ironically. Did he think he'd landed himself the title role in *Father Knows Best*?

Mariah leaned her hip against the desk and wrapped the cord around the binoculars. "Did you find any poachers?"

"I think they were smart enough to head for new territory." He peeled off his well-worn brown leather jacket, which must have been warmer than the fatigue jacket he'd favored earlier. He wore jeans, but this was the first time she had seen him in the gray shirt with the patches and badge that were part of the Forest Service uniform.

"Then maybe you could take me with you this afternoon," Mariah suggested hopefully as she absently unwound the cord again. "Unless you were planning to hang around here the rest of the day."

Hanging around the cabin was a tempting notion. He would be warm and dry and close to Mariah. Which, of course, was the whole problem. Being close. He'd spent two sleepless nights lying on the hard floor of the lookout tower, trying to ignore the voice inside his head that kept telling him how much more comfortable his bed would be—especially with Mariah in it. He wanted to be that close to her, but he knew damn well that even the wanting wasn't a good thing.

"Actually, I was thinking of getting you out of here for the afternoon," he told her. "There's a pretty valley I could show you if you feel up to a short hike. No snow down there, lots of fall colors, a little blue lake."

"Sounds like Camelot," she said, grinning at the prospect as she seated herself on the desk with a springy hop. "Of course I feel up to it. I'm not an invalid—just a little pregnant."

"Just a little?" He'd sworn to himself that he was going to avoid the subject, but he'd hardly thought of anything else. As careful as he'd been all these years, this woman was pregnant. He'd slipped. The knowledge sobered him, humbled him. But it also fascinated him, and her mention of it made him turn up one corner of his mouth in a cocky smile. "I thought there was no such thing."

"Well, as opposed to being 'great with child.' I mean, I'm sure I'm not what they mean by *great* yet." She set the binoculars aside and returned a coy smile for his cocky one. She wanted to be able to talk about it with him, even joke about it. She wanted to be natural. "In other words, I can still walk."

"Pretty steep hike on the way back," he warned.

She knew he wouldn't suggest anything he didn't think she could safely manage. "Lead on."

"Not until we've eaten something." He shook his finger at her. "And I mean *both* of us."

Once they were fed and on their way, Seth took care to break an easy trail, avoiding steep pitches and loose rock. Alone, he would have chosen a more direct route, and he was certain that under ordinary circumstances Mariah could have kept up with him along any route he chose. He could tell by the sure way she handled herself that she was a skilled climber. But he'd also seen that she tired easily, and minimizing risks was foremost on his mind.

As the elevation decreased, so did the snow cover. Golden aspens shimmered in the bright afternoon sun. White-barked birches offered a linear contrast to the broad stippling of low-lying red brush. Seth led the way to a ridge that offered the panoramic view of the lake he had promised. He invited her to perch on a sun-warmed rock, "the best seat in the house," and to visually drink the royal-blue water. Out came the ever-present camera, and he stepped back to line up a shot. She realized after a couple of clicks that, even though a chorus of sparrows and warblers rose above the treetops, she was the only animal in sight. She looked over her shoulder, and the shutter clicked again.

His viewfinder showed him a glorious shot. A friendly breeze lifted her untamed hair, its reddish cast brought to life by the sun. Her chin rested on her shoulder, and a childlike glint of surprise and delight brightened her green eyes.

"No fair!" she complained, laughing. "I wasn't ready."

"I was." He stepped closer and lowered one knee to the ground as he refocused the camera. "Give me that smile again."

"I don't think *Animals All Around Us* will be interested."

"This is for my scrapbook. Pictures of all my visitors."

"Really? Will you show it to me when we get back?"

"There won't be anything in it 'til I get these developed." He lowered the camera and smiled up at her. "I'm a little off the beaten track."

Mariah treasured his smile. Often it seemed shadowed and haunted, but there were times when they would see an animal in the wild, or when he had shown her his pictures—or this moment, sharing the view of the lake— times when his smile was unrestrained and totally engaging.

"Let me take a picture of you," she said, coming down from her perch as she reached for the camera. The look in his eyes became guarded again, but he relinquished the camera. "You sit on the rock," she suggested enthusiastically.

"I like being *behind* the camera much better," he hedged.

"Come on, just relax." She waved her hand as if she were directing a movie shot. "Strike some kind of a rugged mountain-man pose."

"How does that go?" He leaned against the rock and folded his arms.

"Just like that. Now smile," she coaxed as she framed the picture.

"The sun's in my eyes."

"Smile anyway. You look like you're ready to bite me."

He laughed, and she quickly snapped the picture. "Will you send me a copy of that one?" she asked.

She returned the camera, and he turned it over in his

hands, studying the lens for a moment. "What would you do with it?"

"Save it."

He looked up. "For the, uh…for your baby?"

"Yes. Maybe. It depends."

"On what you decide to do?"

"Even if I gave him up for adoption, he might…someday…want to know…"

"Who fathered him." Seth raised one eyebrow, questioning the term. "Or whatever you want to call it."

They looked at each other, and she saw something she hadn't seen in his eyes before. If she trapped one of the wild things he devoted himself to protecting, she imagined she might see such a look in its eyes.

"What would you like him to know about you?" Her question came gently. "Anything?"

"I guess I…" Seth turned away quickly, jamming the camera into its case. "Hell, I don't know. Family medical history, blood type. I wouldn't confuse him with a bunch of sentimental garbage, like pic—"

A flash of green on the crag thirty feet above them caught Seth's eye. He stepped in front of Mariah and unsnapped his holster, leaving his pistol readily accessible.

"What is it?" she asked quietly.

"We've got company," he muttered. "And it smells human to me."

"Hikers?"

"Not likely." He sized up the rock they'd been sitting on, considering it for cover, and surveyed the ten-foot drop-off. The trail was a switchback. If the visitor decided to show himself, he would scramble down an escarpment and appear on the shoulder of the ridge. Seth waited. Within moments, not one but two men, dressed in hunters' camouflage, approached. They ambled down the grade as though they were headed up the steps to ring the doorbell, but each of them carried a combat-style AR-15 automatic rifle on his shoulder.

"You one of Uncle's nephews?" the man in the lead called out, using the old term for a forester in the government's employ.

"I'm with the Forest Service," Seth replied.

"Ranger?"

"Yeah, smoke spotter, game patrol—kind of a jack-of-all-trades up here."

"S'pose you're the only jack they've got up here. Thought most of the stations were closing up for the winter."

Seth stood loose limbed, deceptively relaxed. "Not yet."

"Name's Ray McKenzie." The older man stuck out his hand. "This here's Gordie."

Seth ignored the proffered hand and jerked a nod at the weapon on McKenzie's shoulder. "You got a permit for that thing?"

"Sure do." McKenzie fished in his jacket pockets and produced a battered card, which he handed to Seth. "Just carry it for protection. No game in season yet."

"No kidding."

"We been camping some down below." McKenzie pocketed the permit after Seth returned it. "Sure is pretty up here. Didn't catch your names."

"Cantrell." Seth rested his right hand at his waist just above his pistol. He didn't like the way both men eyed Mariah, waiting. "She's with me."

"Yessir, every hiker ought to have a partner in rugged country like this." McKenzie spat, sending tobacco juice splatting against a rock. He chortled. "Yours is a damn sight prettier than mine, Mr. Cantrell."

"Where are you camped?"

"Oh, we move around. We spend a lot of time in the back country." His toothy grin was speckled with tobacco. "A lot of time. Might say it's gotten to be a way of life with us."

"Is that so? You hunt much, do you?"

"Only in season."

"You strike me as the kind of man who'd be interested in big game."

"Only in season," McKenzie repeated. "I play it by the book."

"There's no season on grizzlies. Not in this neck of the woods."

"Griz can be pretty mean, though. Man's gotta protect himself."

"Man's gotta stay out of their way."

"Yeah, well, this is big country. Not too many men around. That's the way we like it." His grin became a leer when his eyes shifted to Mariah. "But it's nice to see a woman now and again."

Mariah said nothing. The two men gave her the creeps, and she was glad to have the protection Seth's broad back represented. She glanced furtively from the black handle of his holstered pistol to the rifles the two men carried. They could have been headed for a battlefront with weapons like those. Gordie took no more part in the conversation than she did, but he was clearly just a younger version of Ray—wiry body, stubbly beard and a raptor's eyes.

If she could have seen Seth's eyes at that moment, she would have found them even more disturbing. They were the eyes of a male whose territory has been threatened.

"You won't be looking at this one again," Seth said. "She's going home. I suggest you boys do the same. Winter's moving in early."

"Don't worry, Uncle's nephew. I'll look out for mine, and you—" Ray grinned "—you look after yours."

Seth watched the two men scramble over the embankment. They sent a cascade of loose rock rolling toward the timber below.

"Something tells me I'd better be looking over my shoulder for you and yours, you trigger-happy bastard," he grumbled.

Chapter Seven

Seth reported the encounter through the Forest Service dispatcher. He radioed the information he'd memorized from McKenzie's gun permit and described the men. He was told that the sheriff's office would run a check on the permit and let him know if they found any irregularities. In any case, they would get back to him in the morning.

Irregularities. Seth turned the word over in his mind as he stared at the transmitter. Those two hotshots were about as irregular as you could get. The slug he'd cut out of the dead grizzly's shoulder could have been fired from McKenzie's rifle. The weapon wasn't the kind a hunter would ordinarily use, especially not for big game. The AR-15 was a weapon for a showboater, a man who was more interested in playing war games than hunting. The man who carried a semiautomatic rifle, which was easily converted to fully automatic, was either out to hunt people or to fantasize about it. Seth's knowledge came from experience, not from fantasy. He had been a professional soldier, and he'd made no bones about the purpose his weapons had served.

That was all in the past. He was no longer a scout or a point man, just taking orders. Nor was he a hired gun. He was a lookout. His job was to record and report what he saw. That these two were his poachers he had no doubt, and he took the attack against a grizzly in his territory as a personal offense.

Personnel in all phases of forest and wildlife management were stretched pretty thin, and he knew the fires to the south demanded the lion's share of their attention right now. Further, this wasn't the only recent poaching incident. But a *grizzly.* As far as Seth was concerned, the world didn't have grizzlies to spare. They needed his protection.

To protect and defend. By what means? To protect life, a man may have to take life. Who had told him that? Sergeant Mulvaney, he remembered. The first time he'd killed. The first time he had actually seen a man go down under his fire. It had been the one and only time he'd disgraced his uniform with his own vomit. Sergeant Mulvaney, who would have looked more natural in a clerical collar than fatigues, had been there with a canteen. God, that had been a lifetime ago.

But he wasn't a hired gun anymore.

Seth moved to the west window and watched white peaks bathe in the warm glow of the setting sun as they rubbed the underbellies of passing pink and gray clouds. He also had Mariah to think about. He didn't want those creeps so much as laying eyes on her again. He remembered struggling with the seething temptation to knock that wolf leer down McKenzie's throat. Mariah was going to have to go back, he told himself. No two ways about it.

But the thought of being without her didn't sit well with him.

Mariah had supper ready when he got back to the cabin—and that did sit well. The aroma coming from the little stove told him that she had done something remarkable with canned pork. He helped her get the steaming casserole on the table while he listened to her accounting of the dish's ingredients and how she had improvised with canned this and dried that. The challenge his pantry offered seemed to bring out the experimenter in her. Seth didn't really care what was in the dish. It was enough that it tasted fine and warmed his belly, and his enjoyment gave him something to be vocal about. He wasn't ready to broach the other matters that were on his mind.

Neither was Mariah. Food was a neutral topic, and she made a valiant attempt to eat more than her usual portion. Oddly she did it for his sake. Every time he looked up from his plate, she shoveled a forkful of casserole into her mouth. She wanted to please him. She wasn't sure what the presence of the McKenzies meant, but she suspected that she was in the way, a reality that had undoubtedly been confirmed for Seth when he made his report. And she wasn't ready to be sent away.

She asked him no questions; he told her no lies. She was with him tonight, and, like the seasonal huckleberries, she would be gone tomorrow. Enjoy them while you've got the chance, he'd told her when he'd made his offering. He had enjoyed picking them, knowing they were for her. He'd felt like a schoolboy presenting the teacher with an apple he had polished on the seat of his jeans. When Mariah had smiled, he'd felt his face get warm.

They were for the kid, he told himself. The kid whose fate hadn't been decided yet. He had kicked himself for his carelessness at least a hundred times in the past couple of days, but every time he looked at Mariah, he lost touch with all his regrets. The huckleberries were for Mariah, not the baby. She had wished for them, and he wanted her to make wishes that were within his power to grant. A pail of huckleberries. She hadn't asked him for anything else.

He finished his coffee and decided that something stronger was in order tonight. What was done was done. Mariah's future was hers to decide. But she was with him tonight, and, God help him, he wasn't going back to that tower. He wasn't going to leave her alone. He had a family to protect.

Jeez, what dim-witted notion that was! He glanced across the table at her, feeling stupid, wondering if there was any way she could have seen or heard that last wild thought. He caught her toying with her food again.

"I think I'll have a drink," he announced as he cleared his place at the table. "How about you?"

"A drink?"

"I've got some whiskey stashed away for medicinal purposes." He wasn't a teetotaler. She wasn't, either. Why was he manufacturing an excuse?

"Aren't you feeling well?" she asked as she followed suit with her dishes.

"Feeling great." His plate clattered in the dishpan. He added hot water from the stove, then headed for the back room. "Join me?"

"No, thanks. It isn't really good for—" He was out

of sight. She heard some rustling behind the pantry door, and then he was back with an unopened bottle.

"For your health. Right." He rinsed his coffee mug before he broke the seal on the whiskey. "I should know more about those two yokels tomorrow, after the sheriff has a chance to run a check on them. If they decide to send somebody up here to look into this—or even if they don't—I think you'd better plan on going back."

"Tomorrow?" He was wasting no time—not in dealing with her, now that he'd made up his mind, nor in getting to that drink.

"Either way, I can get a chopper up here tomorrow." He gestured toward the dishpan. "I'll clean this up later."

"I'll do them. It'll only take—"

"*I'll* do them." He took his mug and his bottle in one hand and her hand in the other, and led her to the settee. "Later."

"Do you think those men are dangerous?"

"Do I think those men are *dangerous*?" Seth set the bottle on the floor between his feet and sat back, cradling his mug between his hands. She really didn't know. Mariah trusted people. She thought the two men were hunters. A little seedier than most and more than ready to bag their game out of season if the opportunity for "self-defense" presented itself, but she clearly wasn't sure *she* should feel threatened.

Seth remembered how great he'd once thought he looked in camouflage. There had been a time when he couldn't do a job without an M16, or, better yet, an Uzi. His specialty knives had been handmade by a guy in Mexico who custom fit every grip to his customer's hand and ground the sweetest edge on every blade.

His laugh was mirthless. "Honey, I think those men are bona fide loonies."

"I agree." Her responding giggle was innocent and genuine. "They looked like they were dressed for Halloween. They must have bought out the sporting goods store before they came up here."

"Army-Navy surplus." He sipped his whiskey. She'd missed his point, but then, he hadn't made it very well. They were talking out of two different heads, and he sure didn't want her to see what was inside his. Perversely he talked about the McKenzies while he recalled the image he'd once presented to himself in the mirror. "Or you can go through mail-order places that specialize in that kind of stuff."

"You're sending me back because of them?" she asked.

"Partly."

"And the other part?"

"What do you mean, the other part?" He drained his mug and poured again. Fortified, he was able to level an emotionless stare. "Look, you've had a few days to sort things out. A lot of solitude, nobody pressuring you. Now I've got things to do."

"I see."

The words came like two little jabs at his chest, forcing him to search for some mitigating explanation. "It's crazy, you being up here. It's no good for you, no good for me. All I can think about is—" He looked down at the blue mug. "You know. Just the fact that you're here."

"I think it *has* been good for me," she differed quietly. "I needed to talk, and you've let me...some."

"Not enough?" He took another drink and angled toward her, hooking his arm over the back of the settee.

"You've got the rest of the night, then, honey. Talk all you want."

"I want you to talk, too. I was thinking in terms of *discussion*."

"About what? Kids? I never had any. Last time I spent much time around kids was—" He studied the hand he'd rested on the top of the backrest, and he remembered the way he'd first earned his calluses by hauling hay bales. "When I lived on the farm. I think I might have been a kid myself then."

"I'm sure you were."

"But that was a hell of a long time ago," he averred, getting back to his drink.

"Sometimes..." She scooted closer, just a little, because she had the oddest sense that if she crowded him, she would scare him away. "Sometimes—like the time you showed me those pictures of the squirrel, and you told me how he got into your backpack—sometimes I can see the child in you."

"There's no child in me."

"Yes, there is, Seth. There's one in all of us."

"In you, maybe." He raised his mug in salute to her. "In you, certainly. Not me. If there ever was one, I killed it the first time I—" He saw the sudden cloudiness in her eyes, the pursed mouth, and he wanted to bite his tongue. "Poor choice of words. I didn't mean...I make no judgments, Mariah. I've got no right. You do what you have to do."

"You have a right to say how you feel."

"No." Her suggestion struck him as outrageous, and it came in a disarmingly quiet voice. And if, indeed, he had such a right, what would he say? "I don't 'feel' a whole lot. I just live and let live. That's the best I can do."

"What *did* you mean, then?" she coaxed. "About killing the child in you."

"I meant—" He had to work a little bit to remember. The whiskey was doing its job, lulling his brain. "You were talking about innocence, and I can hardly remember what that means. When I went to 'Nam, I remember thinking I was somehow going to make life better for those people, that they would thank me for it." His mind cleared. It always did when he recalled those faces. "They didn't."

"Neither did the people at home."

He raised his hand to stop her. "Hey, I'm not looking for any sympathy on that score. I just…I got to be pretty good at my job when I was over there. Pretty efficient. When you do what I did, and you do it well, nobody thanks you for it. When the job is over, you take your pay, and you move on to the next one."

"What kind of job did you do?"

He looked at her and wondered how much she really wanted to know. How much could she accept, and how much did he need to tell her?

"I was a soldier, that's all. I carried a gun, and I used it. That was my job."

"I'm sure you weren't in it for the money. Especially not in those days. They didn't pay—"

"The U.S. government didn't pay me very well, but other governments did. I got my training in the marines. I put it to use and made a damn good living later on."

"You were…like a mercenary?"

"Yeah. Like that." He tossed down what was left in the cup. "Only we don't like the term 'mercenary.' We prefer 'specialist' or 'professional soldier,' or maybe 'advisor.'" She was leaning closer, fascinated, and he had half a notion to make it sound so damn romantic that she would crawl into his lap and tell him how brave he was. "I was a soldier of fortune." He chuckled, mostly at the irony of his stupid notion. "I always liked the sound of that term."

"That's how you ended up in Central America."

"And that's where I got malaria." She hadn't crawled into his lap yet. The malaria used to get them every time. But then, Mariah had seen it firsthand, which kind of took the edge off the mystique. "So now you know the rest of the story."

"I have a feeling I don't know the half of it."

"Smart girl." He poured himself another drink.

"And I couldn't know—not really—not even if you told me every detail," she said as she watched him raise the cup toward his lips.

He caught that earnest look in her eyes, and the cup came down slowly. "Just like I can't know—not really— what it's like to be in your shoes." He reached for her, touching her cheek with the backs of his fingers. In a raspy voice he added, "With the baby inside you."

"I think—" Mariah drew a shaky breath. "I think we're comparing apples and oranges."

"No." He withdrew his touch and went back to drinking his whiskey. "We're comparing death with life. There's probably a connection somewhere."

"We're talking about your life and mine," she said anxiously. "You don't have anything to do with death anymore."

"I've meted out a lot of it."

"You make yourself sound quite powerful, as if it's for you to decide."

"Hell, when I'm pulling the trigger, who else is deciding? If somebody'd shot me the day I stepped off that first troop transport, how many other people would be alive? Mariah, I have—''

He closed his eyes. *I have killed.* Oh, God, he hadn't said that yet. Not to her. Not to the woman who'd quickened his seed. There he went again, thinking about this as if it were going to be some blessed event. The fact was that he'd screwed up again, and people were going to pay for it. Lives would be affected.

''I have done things, Mariah.'' He forced his eyes open and grabbed her wrist, commanding every shred of her attention. ''If you knew about them, you'd hate the fact that you'd been touched by these hands. You'd feel defiled, and you'd feel nothing for me but contempt. Do you understand? In a face-off between Ray McKenzie and me, you'd stand behind *him*. You'd ask him to protect you from me. If you were smart, you'd be afraid of me.''

Mariah turned her wrist within the tight cuff of his grip. ''Why?''

''Because of what I've been.'' He slid closer, and she tried to draw her arm away. ''You *are* afraid of me, aren't you? I've already messed up your life so badly—''

''Seth—''

''I can't undo it, but maybe I can...'' His eyes went soft with his petition. ''Don't be afraid of me, Mariah. I won't hurt you anymore.''

''You haven't—''

''I promise you. I want to hold you again. You like it when I hold you.''

''Yes, I do.''

He set the whiskey away from him and took a gentler hold on her shoulders. ''I don't want you to be afraid of me. Ever. I'll back off whenever you say, but if nothing else, I know I can give you—''

"I'm not afraid of you, Seth. I never have been."

"Then let me give you this."

It was only a fraction of what she wanted from him, but his kiss felt so hard and hungry that she couldn't quite remember what else there was. And it was good. Lord, it was good to taste the honey of his tongue again when it came searching, seeking a playmate. He pulled her into his lap and made love to her mouth with his spearing tongue.

In the midst of their kissing Mariah shifted to straddle his lap, and the contact they made then brought a needy groan from deep in his throat. Liquid heat slowly spread through Mariah's body. She slid her tongue against his, then slid away and lightly sucked its tip. She held the power of his shoulders in her hands, and the measured skill of his hands massaged her back, her buttocks, and then the sides of her breasts.

He knew she wore no bra beneath her soft flannel shirt. He knew his thumbs would have free access to whisk the loose fabric against her nipples and make them tighten. He spared a little manipulation for the buttons of her shirt and brought her breasts out of hiding. They rose and fell softly in the shadows, like two sheltered cubs waiting to be attended to. He cupped them in his hands and touched his lips to one pouting nipple.

"Do they hurt?" he whispered. "I've heard—"

"They feel a little—" She sucked in a breath, lifting them higher. "I want you to touch them."

"Are you sure?" Her moan seemed affirmative. "I'll go easy."

He touched her nipple with the tip of his tongue, and the sharp catch in her breath startled him. But she didn't flinch, and when he hesitated, she threaded her fingers into his hair and held his face to her breast. He ministered to it with exquisite tenderness, spreading his tongue to soothe, then spiking it to tease. She rocked her hips against him, almost imperceptibly at first, but the motion mounted. Soon she was riding him hard, and he felt as though he would surely burst if he didn't bury himself inside her. His pants locked him in, and he was hard-pressed to get out. He savored the tang of anticipation.

Mariah fumbled with the buttons of his shirt, and he raised his head to kiss her. Yes, he would be naked for her now. He would be everything she needed tonight. "Wanna go to bed with me?" he whispered, nuzzling her.

"Yes."

"Hang on. I'll give you a lift."

He pressed her knees against his sides, slid his hands around her buttocks and stood almost effortlessly. With the first step he knocked the tin mug over with the toe of his boot, but neither of them seemed to notice. Mariah nibbled his ear and promised, "In return for the lift, I'll undress you and tuck you in."

"Tuck me in where?"

"A small, warm bed," she whispered. "Like a cradle. And I'll rock you, massage you, make all your muscles relax."

"Fine." As he reached the bed, he wondered how long it had been since a woman's softly spoken promise had made him so hard. "But not 'til I've given you so damn much pleasure you're busting at the seams."

She could tell that her passion pitched his to new heights, but he refused to lose control. His touch was breathtaking, but his exquisite tenderness made her heart ache along with her breasts and her belly. He made her want his touch first, and then he followed a sixth sense as he gave it to her, meeting every need with just the right pressure, just the right motion. He knew when she was nearly mindless, when to part her athlete's thighs gone limp and use his artful tongue to make her all sensation. She tensed as some reservation occurred to her, but his mastery had been established. "Seth..." she whispered.

"Don't turn me away, Mariah," he whispered, letting just his breath warm her belly. "Give me this moment to make you happy."

He loved the sound of his name on her tongue and the taste of her on his. When he knew he could wait no longer, he let her tuck him inside her and make him as happy as he had made her, and they shared that window of time that could no more be measured than it could be stopped or stored or saved.

Seth caressed the soft hollow at the back of Mariah's knee, then took hold of her there and drew her leg up around his hip. "Great legs." He explored her muscular calf with an appreciative hand, letting the fine stubble tickle his palm. He smiled in the dark, thinking of all the inconveniences a woman had to put up with when she was "roughing it" that a man wouldn't know anything about. The soft fuzz and the shapely calf felt heart-meltingly feminine under his callused hand. "I suppose you hear that a lot," he added absently.

"From my coach," she admitted. She was making her own acquaintance with the curves and planes of his chest. "When he thinks I'm in peak condition."

"Oh yeah?" He pressed his hand against her skin and rubbed slowly. "How does he make that assessment?"

"He charts power curves—power versus speed—watches for the balance of power on my right and left sides. Keeps track of my poling power."

"Sounds like a real diplomat. Let me see if we've got a balance of power here," he teased as he slid his other hand along her other thigh.

"You're comparing calf to thigh there."

"Am I?" He shifted to his hip, and his hand followed the back of her thigh to her buttocks. "I'll bet this part has something to do with it, too."

"The thighbone's connected to the…hipbone," she recited in a low, sexy voice. Then she switched to an impersonal tone. "We do some weight training, but I don't have to be muscle-bound. It's a balance between strength and endurance. Oxygen intake, efficient use of energy— the coach watches all those things."

"On paper?"

"Not *just* on paper."

"I mean, he doesn't have to be running his hands over you checking for little pockets of fat, does he?"

"No, he doesn't check for *little pockets of fat*."

"Good." He memorized her with a light touch. "Good," he repeated softly. He was teasing, but the idea of someone else's hands taking inventory of her muscles irked him.

"What are *you* checking for?"

"Whatever you've got." His fingertips skated over her hip, and he pictured what he could only feel. "Dimples, moles, scars." He nibbled at her ear and confided as he touched the inner curve of her knee, "You need a shave."

"I know." He had noticed, she thought. Damn. She wanted whatever she had to be beautiful now. "I didn't bring a razor."

"It feels kinda nice." He made small circles with his fingertips. "Like a little chick, just hatched."

She drew her knee up and scooted closer, stopping

short of pressing her hips against him. In the hollow between their bellies she could feel his heat, sense his slow pulsing. "Ah, the farm boy comes out in you."

He gave a low, lusty chuckle. "Watch who you're calling a boy, woman, or I'll give you another taste of *my* poling power."

"Is that a threat or a promise?"

They hugged each other with arms and legs and laughter, and she pinched his side. "What's this?" she exclaimed. "A little pocket of fat?"

"Hell, no." Seth rolled on his back, taking Mariah with him, belly to belly. "Find it now," he challenged.

She looked for handles at his sides and found none. He slipped his hand between them, sliding it over her flat belly. "And what's this?" he whispered.

The joviality faded like an echo in the mountains. "It's likely to become sort of a…big pocket of…"

"Not fat," he said.

"No, but a big pocket…if I let it."

His hand stirred to soothe her. "Have you decided?" he asked quietly. He needed to know.

"Yes. No." She tried to slide away from him, but he held her close and kept his hand where it was. She pressed her forehead against his shoulder and whispered, "I don't know, Seth."

"Are you afraid of your father?"

"No." She turned her head and laid her cheek against his warm skin. Comfort. "It's just that…I usually end up taking his advice."

"No one can make you abort your pregnancy, Mariah."

"I know that."

"I'm not trying to convince you either way," he said. "Whatever's right for you." He meant what he said, but he knew he harbored a hope, and he cursed himself for it. When had he stopped shunning the kind of complications for which relationships, all human relationships, were famous? Poets and songwriters played them to the hilt. Mind-bending complications. How in hell could he lie here and make these crazy statements? But they kept coming. "I'd like to help."

"How do you really feel about it?" she asked.

"I don't think I have any rights in this. I just thought maybe I could—"

"I want to know how you feel about the baby, Seth."

"I'm not used to feeling much of anything." Holding her like this more than stretched his limits.

"You're human. It's there somewhere."

"Yeah, maybe." That was what they had told him in the hospital. The feelings were in there somewhere. It had made him angry to hear them say that over and over, smug as hell, as if their licenses and degrees gave them X-ray vision into the workings of his mind. "But I'm not your father. I'm not gonna try to tell you what you should do."

"You're the baby's—"

"It's not really a baby yet, is it? I mean—" He closed his eyes and tried to imagine what was just a few layers of skin and muscle beneath his hand. "Jeez, Mariah, when I think of it I get—"

She felt the almost imperceptible stirring of his fingertips. "So do I," she whispered.

"Not mushy," he said quickly, even though his tone belied his words. "I'm not getting dewy-eyed over this."

"No, of course not."

"It's just that I was always pretty careful."

"Even when you were married?"

"Yeah. Even then."

"Why?"

"It wasn't much of a marriage." He put both arms around her. He wasn't sure how much he was about to tell her, but in the mood he was in, he was afraid he might go overboard and drive her away. He wanted her close. "I was between wars. Thought I wanted to settle down. Took the first opportunity. Got married in a fever, as the saying goes."

"Isn't that when the first baby usually comes along before the first wedding anniversary?"

"We figured we'd wait 'til I got a decent job. I tried construction, worked for a farm implement dealer—pretty soon I was climbing the walls from sheer boredom. It was kinda like going from driving race cars to delivering the mail. After what I'd gotten used to in 'Nam, I guess I couldn't feel alive unless my life was on the line."

"So how did you get into…your other line of work."

"My *other* line of work?" He sighed. She was going to drag it out of him, he thought, and then he had to admit that he wanted to tell her. "I answered an ad. They were looking for an 'assault specialist,' and I knew I fit the bill. I got in with a group of vets, and we hired out as professional soldiers. Eventually I went solo."

"And your wife?"

"She found ways to entertain herself back home."

"Why did you quit?"

"I'd been at it for about three years, coming home now and then for a week or two at a time. Finally the whole thing was kinda getting to me—I was strung tighter than a fiddle, ducking every time somebody lit a match—and I came home, thinking I just needed rest.…

"Carla didn't even pretend she was glad to see me." He sighed and remembered that he had stopped blaming

Carla for what she had done. After all, he hadn't been entirely faithful, either. But in those days he had been *the man*, and if anyone had accused him of harboring a double standard, he would have told them where to perch. Now he had his own life to live, and he didn't claim the right to cast stones at his ex-wife.

"Things got pretty tense between us," he continued simply. "I was suspicious, hostile, paranoid, you name it. Carla just said I was crazy."

"Did you...were you violent?"

"I didn't abuse her physically, if that's what you mean. But verbally...yeah, I could get pretty violent. Not only that, the relapses were worse then, and she couldn't take it when I'd hallucinate. Anyway, she walked. And I spent eight months in a VA hospital."

He'd mentioned nightmares that had nothing to do with malaria, and Mariah had heard about delayed stress syndrome, an emotional problem many Vietnam veterans experienced. Seth was a strong, private man, and she knew it cost him heavily to expose this much of himself to her. She held him and waited for whatever he would tell her.

"It all came back to me, you know? All the dead men and the bleeding women and the crying babies. It was like this little brush fire that I'd managed to contain suddenly blew up in my face. Instant forest fire, only it was a forest full of burning bodies, and I was in the middle of it. Hell, I'd torched them myself."

"You must have been hurting for such a long time."

"I couldn't shake the memory of this one kid," he said quietly. "I was part of a scout team." She didn't need to know just how specialized his training had been, how deadly his efficiency. But he wanted her to know what he'd done. The worst of it were the women and children, and how he'd managed to dehumanize them in his mind, blow them away like so much dust. There was no rhyme or reason to it, but suddenly he needed a woman's forgiveness. *This* woman's forgiveness.

"We'd go into a village in VC territory sometimes just to take out one or two targeted people. Pretty risky. Most of the time we were in and out before anyone knew it, but there was this one time…there was this kid—this baby, really—and he got in the way of…" In his mind he saw the child, and then the destruction of the child, and he knew he'd told Mariah all he could.

"That's over, Seth," she whispered. "It was a terrible time, but it's over. You aren't to blame for it."

"What I did," he began hesitantly. "I see it in my mind, over and over, and I know it didn't have to be…the way it was. I got to the point…you know, I kept telling myself it was me or them. And I believed it. And I…killed some people…"

"It's all over, Seth," she whispered. "That's all behind you. Let it go."

He hugged her close. His soft-spoken madonna. His throat burned, and it was a long time before he could speak again. "If I could help you somehow," he said, his voice raspy at first, "if there was anything I could do, Mariah, anything you'd let me do…I mean, if you decide not to…"

"I have decided," she told him. "I'm going to have the baby."

The news struck him like a thunderbolt.

"You know, I think I was just trying to let time run out," she confessed. "I needed to get out of my dad's reach for a while so I wouldn't have to hear all his perfectly good reasons, and I guess I wanted to get far enough along in my pregnancy that I'd have to carry it to term. But that's the coward's way out. I've made my decision. If I can't…well, there are plenty of people who want to…adopt new—'' He heard her swallow convulsively. She took a deep breath and rushed on. "Newborn babies.''

He felt warm inside, honored just to be able to hold her. "It must be nice to be able to give life," he whispered. "I destroyed so damn much of it that I finally—I guess I finally flipped out.''

There was more, and he wanted her to know that. Good things that had come after the bad. "After I got out of the hospital, I went to school and took up forestry. I spent some time in the mountains. I found peace here, and life that needed protecting. Protecting is one thing, but making life happen…''

"You had something to do with it, too, Seth.''

"I was just…in the right place at the right time.''

"Funny," she said with a smile. "A few days ago, you probably would have said just the opposite.''

He made a clucking sound in his cheek. "I might not have said it, but I know I thought it.''

"And now?''

"Now…'' He touched her firm belly again. "Now I like knowing there's part of me…here, inside you…and that you want it to live and grow.'' He wanted her to tell him that she wanted to be his child's mother, too, but he knew that was too much. He knew she really wanted to keep the baby, but the fact that it was his had nothing to do with it. He was just some guy she'd ended up with one crazy night, and she'd gotten caught. He was glad she didn't hate him for it.

And it was too much for Mariah to hope that Seth would tell her that he wanted to help her raise this baby. He'd offered to help—at one point he'd said financially.

But that this mountain maverick might entertain the notion of being a father was just so much romantic nonsense.

Loving him was, too.

Chapter Eight

Seth zipped his leather jacket against the crisp morning cold and pulled on a pair of split cowhide work gloves. From the lookout tower's catwalk he saw tranquility that seemed inviolate. The sun had just risen in the saddle between two mountains, casting the snowcapped peaks in crimson and gold. There was so much space with so blessedly few people, but he knew the tranquility was deceptive. It was likely that somewhere out there two gun-happy human vultures were still lurking.

He scanned the distant ridges as if trying to confirm his concerns with the naked eye. Maybe the sheriff's office would turn up something on those two this morning, preferably a reason to arrest them. They weren't even adept at poaching, couldn't even manage a clean kill. But he'd seen other men like Ray McKenzie—same dress, same toys, same attitude. If, as Seth suspected, Ray and Gordie were a couple of those radicals who called themselves survivalists and took to the wilderness to avoid the imminent calamity their movement liked to predict, they were going to be hard-pressed to hold up their end of the battle. They'd botched their shot at the grizzly and missed the rams completely. But being incompetent didn't make them any less menacing. Seth wanted them out of his area.

He settled his hands on his hips and stretched one shoulder at a time, then tilted his head first to the left, then to the right. It had been one hell of a night. Even after Mariah had drifted off to sleep, he'd kept his promise to hold her. He had a stiff neck, but the memory of waking up next to her brought a smile to his face. He took a deep breath. The scent of pine and the sight of mist dissipating with the rising sun and the thought of Mariah in his bed—Lord, what a morning!

Off to the south stood Crawford Mountain. Who would have thought notoriously unsociable Seth Cantrell would let a woman into his secluded life and name one of his mountains after her? He could imagine the craggy peak laughing at him. Trees would tremble then, and rocks would roll.

The larches and spruce trees covered the lower slopes. Great place to get lost, Seth mused as he took in the view. A man could disappear forever up here, especially if nobody down below had reason to look for him. A woman could, too, if she had no ties and a lot of gumption. She would have a good chance if she had a man to protect her. One man, one woman, one forest.

If she had no ties. Pretty tough for a world-class athlete bound for the U.S. Nordic Ski Team to disappear. But if she had help, he reasoned, the right kind of help, she might pull it off. A mental voice sounding suspiciously conscientious told him that he wasn't the right kind of help, considering the selfish motive he was doing his damnedest to ignore. But he beat the voice back with an insistence that he was clearly the man for the job. If this woman didn't want to be found, he could see to it that she wasn't.

He'd left her sleeping, that unruly auburn hair laying claim to his pillow. Mariah, whose name reminded him of a warm wind. Her face recalled for him the innocence he'd lost so long ago he couldn't count the time. Her body, warm and soft this morning and smelling of sex and sleep, offered safe harbor and sustenance. She had shared it with him, and he'd wondered at the feeling of being welcome inside her. But the child—*his* child, and that was the real wonder—depended upon that small taut belly for its very life.

He had been the one to point out to Mariah that no one could make her abort her pregnancy, and he believed that. It was her decision—simple as that. Simple if you weren't the one who had to make it. He knew what it meant to seek solitude, to get away from all the noise and try to come to terms with the way things really were. Maybe the need to disappear came to everyone sooner or later. At first you felt like a coward, but once you'd managed to leave all the trappings of your former life behind and make peace with yourself—God, what bliss. You weren't hurting anyone, and they couldn't hurt you. Nobody could get to you mentally who couldn't get to you physically. That was why Mariah had come.

And that was why he wanted to let her stay.

Seth gripped the binoculars that hung around his neck and started to lift them, then stopped. Who was he kidding? He didn't have it in him to be any woman's champion. There were a hundred good reasons for sending her back now, and surely only one for letting her stay. One self-serving, archaic reason. A man's needs.

He looked down at the cabin and pictured her in his bed, turning in her sleep toward the side where he'd slept. He was no savior, but neither was he some marauder who stashed women in his cabin to meet the demands of his sexual appetite. Mariah was vulnerable to him now, and he knew that what he was really considering, bottom line, was using that vulnerability to his advantage. What else could it be?

He stood with his legs apart and the binoculars held stiffly, the move to lift them suspended, forgotten. He knew he ought to send for a helicopter without any more delay. Turning slowly, he looked back through the huge window and eyed the radio. Why couldn't he make the call?

As if on cue, the radio crackled and came to life, beckoning him with his call letters.

A short time later, Seth let himself into the cabin and found Mariah looking much as he'd pictured her. He moved quietly, and she didn't stir until he sat on the bed beside her and lifted her hair away from her face. She smiled before she opened her eyes.

"Is it time to get up?"

He chuckled and spoke softly. "I've been up for hours, woman. You must have been partying all night or something."

"Entertaining." The word seemed to disturb him. She laid her hand on his thigh and amended, "Celebrating. I think I celebrated into the wee hours."

"Special occasion?" He combed his fingers through her hair.

"Mmm, I thought it was. Very special."

"I thought so, too." He liked the way her hair curled around his fingers like static-charged satin. "I didn't want to leave you this morning, but I was expecting a call."

"Did it come?" she wondered as she stretched one arm.

He nodded.

The arm came down. "And did you tell on me?"

He laughed and ruffled her hair. "No, I did not tell on you. Why would I do a thing like that?"

She smiled saucily and insinuated her head into his lap like a cat that wanted stroking. "Because you want to get me out of your hair?"

"Who's in whose hair?"

She sighed, snuggled and closed her eyes while he stroked the hair she knew to be a wild mess. She didn't care. "I'm happy right where I am."

"I'm happy where you are, too." She giggled and rubbed her forehead against the fly of his jeans. "Mmm, yes, make yourself comfortable. But as far as the roof over your head goes, ah!" He shifted slightly. Her maneuvers were gaining on him. "It won't be long before I have to shut the station down for the winter, and then we'll figure something else out."

She looked up at him. "We will?"

"I want to help you. I want to do what I can. You'll just have to tell me what that is."

"You mean my wish is your command?"

"Something like that."

She sat up and made a production of plumping pillows, while Seth watched her breasts jiggle. "Breakfast in bed?"

"Sure."

"For both of us?" She reached for the closest shirt, which happened to be the one he'd taken off and dropped beside the bed the night before. "I'll make yours, and you make mine."

"I'll be getting the better end of the deal."

"We'll see." As she swung her legs off the side of the bed, she began buttoning the shirt. "Where do you spend your winters?"

"Depends on what I want to photograph," he said absently, watching her dress, as though something delicious was being swallowed up by someone else. "*Great Outdoors* is looking for something on caribou, so I thought I'd head up to Canada. Might get some good wolf shots while I'm at it." She didn't look up, but the progress she'd been making on the buttons slowed dramatically. "Of course, my plans are always flexible this time of year."

"I'm thinking of doing some substitute teaching," she tossed out lightly as she picked up her buttoning speed. "There's always a shortage of subs—always enough work to keep you busy."

Seth rose from the bed. "Sounds like an idea." Not the one he wanted to hear, but a reasonable one. He headed for the stove, his eye on the blue metal coffeepot. "Can you handle your dad?"

"I think so," Mariah said as she padded across the floor after him.

"What about your coach?"

"He's told me a dozen times that if I don't fill that slot on the team, someone else will." He'd taken the pot off the shelf, and she held out her hand. "I'll make coffee if you'll stoke up that fire."

Relinquishing the pot, he gave her toes a nod. "You oughta get something on those feet and—" he grinned at the sight of her goose bumps "—those legs."

"I thought you enjoyed seeing my legs," she pouted.

"I do, but without the goose bumps."

"Then let's have a roaring fire."

They stared at each other for a moment. The stoking had already begun.

"Can you stay a few more days?" Seth asked, almost shyly.

Mariah smiled. "I can stay as long as I'm welcome."

"How soon before your dad starts looking for you?"

The question erased her smile. She glanced down at the coffeepot and stepped back from him. "Let me get some water and get this going."

He watched her disappear quickly into the back room. "He *will* be looking for you, then."

"Probably soon," came the answer.

"I know you're an important commodity and all that, but at this point in your life, you ought to be able to—"

She was back with the water, and the look in her eyes cut him off. "Commodity is kind of a…mercenary word."

"I guess it is."

Seth took care of the fire in silence. His choice of words had been cold, but he suspected it was accurate. Still, he wished he hadn't said it. Obviously it had cut deep, and that wasn't what he wanted to be doing. Not now.

Mariah put the coffee on the stove and took her own thoughts to the back room, where she washed and dressed. How could a person be a commodity? Get real, she told herself. Sports is business, with the athlete being the stock in trade. Not that she was involved in a high profile sport like football, but she had reached the screaming point more than once. This is *me*, flesh and blood Mariah Crawford. This is *my* life. And lately her too often cloudy identity had seemed even more crucial.

This is *my* baby. How could her father or Seth or anyone else know who she was if she didn't take a stand?

Seth was half kneeling on the hearth, watching the flames. "I need to cut some more wood pretty soon," he announced without looking up when Mariah returned.

She brought two cups of black coffee, and he joined her on the settee. "You're right," she told him as she handed him the steaming mug. "It's time I let my father know that all the nagging in the world won't change anything. This is not my year to make the ski team. It's my year to have a baby."

He sipped his coffee, then watched the steam from his cup curl into oblivion. "I shouldn't ask you—shouldn't even *let* you stay." He rested the tin mug against his thigh and enjoyed the heat for a moment before he looked at her to explain. "The sheriff's office ran a check on those gun permits. The Ray McKenzie who owned that permit died last summer. The other permit was stolen from somebody named Gordon Schott. Both permits had been pretty skillfully altered."

"Who do you think they could be? Criminals of some kind?"

"The kind who carry false permits at the very least." With a sigh he added, "The kind who carry assault weapons for God knows what reason."

"They're probably gone by now. They knew you were on to them."

"Maybe." He wanted it to be true, and he figured there was enough doubt to allow him to hedge. "The sheriff's checking with the feds. Might turn up something from the description I gave. Game warden's coming back this afternoon. We'll take another run, see if we can spot them. I'd love to have them match that slug up with

McKenzie's rifle.'' He lifted one shoulder indifferently. ''Or whatever the bastard's name is.''

''He could always say the bear attacked him,'' Mariah pointed out.

''Yeah, I know. That's why I didn't accuse him of anything. Didn't want to give him the satisfaction of coming up with some cock-and-bull story. Of course, if you wound an animal, you're supposed to find a ranger or a warden and report it, which he didn't do. But when it's man against grizzly, people tend to side with the man.''

This was what really interested him, she told herself. This was his great love. ''There have been so many horror stories.''

''People often bring the attacks that do happen on themselves. And there haven't been that many. It's just that they make such good press.'' He relaxed visibly with his coffee, taking a sip and settling back, taking another one. ''We're supposed to be the ones with the superior intelligence,'' he said, gesturing with his cup. ''People think bears are cute. They want them to be stuffed with cotton.''

''Well, the cubs—''

''The cubs are the most dangerous. Where there's a cub, there's a mama, and she ain't too cute when she's angry, let me tell you.''

Mariah raised her brow. ''Have you gotten too close?''

''I spent several hours treed by a silvertip sow once. Bears can climb trees, you know. She could have had my butt if she'd wanted it, but I think she got some perverse female thrill out of making me sweat. She just kind of hung around eating berries and keeping an eye on her cubs, who were playing in the stream nearby. Every time I moved, she stood up on her hind legs and flashed her claws. Finally she let me know I wasn't worth her trouble. She yawned.'' He shook his head, remembering the way he'd been kicking himself for his own stupidity by that time, and the bear had confirmed it. ''I swear I could hear her laughing at me when she turned and ambled away.''

It was hard to imagine Seth sitting in a tree. ''You were lucky.''

''Hell of it was, my camera was on the ground the whole time. Her parting insult was to flatten it with one well-placed paw.'' He whacked his hand against his thigh to show how it was done.

Mariah nodded at his demonstration. ''That could have been your head.''

''There's always that risk.'' Like the ranger giving a lecture to a tenderfoot, as he'd done on occasion, he raised a warning finger. ''If you're going to go looking for grizzlies, you've got a responsibility not to provoke them. Most people can't resist doing something stupid around them. Most people should stay the hell away from them and let them be wild.''

''Why can't you?'' Mariah challenged him.

'''Cause I'm crazy.'' He checked her eyes for a reaction and found only that she was listening, waiting for an answer she could believe. ''And because they need me. They need a buffer, somebody to come between them and civilization, which gets closer to crowding them out with every year that passes.''

''Why you?''

''Why not? I've got this wildness in me that isn't going to go away. I might as well use it for something good.'' ''Good'' was a term he'd lost touch with for a time, but now the coffee tasted good, and he felt good, sitting there beside Mariah. ''I think it's a good thing, protecting the bears," he said earnestly. Then he looked to her for much-needed affirmation. "Don't you?"

"I think there's too little wildness left." She nodded, smiling at him tenderly. "I think it has to be protected by those who understand it."

"Do you understand it?"

"I think wild things are delicate, and dangerous. You thrive on both. You cherish what's fragile, and you seek the presence of danger once in a while. Risk-taking is what makes you tick."

"I'd have made a hell of a bullfighter."

"I suspect you're a hell of a ranger. And I'm sure you were a good soldier."

Oh, God, *that*. He studied the last third of his cup of coffee. "They told me I was. They gave me the medals to prove it."

"But things must have gotten out of hand." She hesitated, knowing she was treading on sensitive ground. "Frankly, I can't imagine a war happening any other way."

His mouth hardened for a moment as he stared at her. "You can't imagine having a war, period." She flinched, and he told himself she shouldn't have to. He set the cup aside and reached for her hand, apologizing with his eyes. "You can't, Mariah," he said quietly. "I hope you never have to know." He pressed his lips to the center of her palm and breathed the soft scent of guiltlessness. "A woman like you should never, ever—"

"We're not so different, Seth. I like to be tested. I enjoy a challenge." He closed his hand around hers and let her innocence speak to him of what she supposed they had in common. "And many times," she continued convincingly, "I do what I'm told, even if it isn't exactly what I want to do. You must have had to do that, too."

"You're an athlete."

"I'm also a woman. When I'm training or competing, I listen to the experts because I want to be good at what I'm doing. For me, it's a matter of winning. For you, it was survival."

"I had some ideas about winning, too."

"But sometimes—" She set her cup aside and angled her body toward his. Their knees touched. "Sometimes we go overboard. We all need balance in our lives. We need to be human."

"That's the fragile part." Like the hand he was holding. He didn't care what her "poling power" was, her hand felt small and precious in his. "That's the part I couldn't live with anymore."

"But you can now."

"I don't know."

"But you do! Look around you," she ordered with a sweeping gesture. "These mountains, all this wilderness. It looks rugged and indomitable, but it's not. It's fragile. If they take away trees, or water, or grass, or even predators, the balance is gone." Her hand came to rest on his thigh. "You're that way, too. You *are* rugged, but you're the gentlest, most sensitive man—"

"Compared to who?"

She saw the disbelief in his dark eyes, and she shrugged. "Compared to Albert Schweitzer. I don't know. Compared to anybody." Her hand stirred against the soft, worn denim. "You know, Seth, I haven't had time to get close to very many people. I don't have too many friends. It seemed important to me that we be friends."

He glanced at the hand that promised to distract him from the direction their conversation was taking. "Yeah, I guess I can see why it would, under the circumstances."

"That's the way it started, but even without the—" she squirmed a little and took her hand away "—circumstances...I'm glad I know you now."

They shared the silence, taking time to consider the circumstances. Seth no longer thought of them as complications. He was bound up in her life now, and he had stopped thinking that she was complicating his. What they shared felt suspiciously like friendship, or something even worse.

"I haven't had any friends in a long time." He ran his thumb over her small round knuckles. "I guess I'm not a very friendly man."

"It would be hard to find too many friends up here."

"Mountain goats," he teased. "I know plenty of mountain goats." He'd given her something to smile about, and she'd taken him up on it, even though it wasn't that funny. "But not many people. It seemed to make life simpler just to be by myself."

"You must have had friends. Didn't you have friends in the army?"

He drew a long, slow breath. Just generally, he told himself. That was all she was asking. "In the army, you're damned if you do and damned if you don't. You want somebody you can trust at your back, but you get too close... They get blown away, and you're blown away with them." That's all, he told himself. That's enough.

But the story tumbled out of him, slowly at first. "I had a buddy. He was from West Virginia." The introduction brought a wistful smile to Seth's lips, and the glaze of memory settled over his eyes. "Biggest, clumsiest hillbilly who ever walked the earth. Talked real slow, lahk he warn't never in no hurry ta git 'is stowry tole."

The imitation was funny coming from Seth, but there was something ominous about it. Mariah's smile was tentative. "What was his name?"

"Hugh Sleeper." He chuckled fondly. "What a name. Big Hughy. Said his Uncle Sam named the big Huey helicopter after him but didn't know how to spell it right. That was about his best joke, too. But when he had a job to do, he did it with such finesse. Slick, clean, noiseless."

Seth chose not to elaborate on that; she didn't need to know that it was the highest praise for the kind of killing the scout team had been assigned to do. Big Hughy would have been pleased with the compliment, and he would have approved of the lack of detail in front of a lady. "Anyway, he was somebody you could count on, no matter what was goin' down."

Enough, he told himself again. She asked you if you had any friends in the army, and you told her. But those green eyes seemed to welcome every word and invite more, and out they came. Unconsciously he pressed his knee more tightly against hers.

"Then one night…it was early morning, really. That still, quiet time just before dawn. We were coming back from a mission, and ol' Hughy was ticked, and I mean, he let me know it. I'd almost blown the whole party by letting my, uh…well, my man—my target—I didn't get him fast enough, and that meant we had to…
It got to be a pretty tight situation. And Hugh liked a clean job, so he was—"

He'd been staring at a spot beyond Mariah's head, but suddenly he laughed and looked at her again, inviting her to enjoy the humor. "He called me a dumb farmer. Can you believe it? That was about the meanest he could manage. And then he stretched those long legs of his and left me to bring up the rear, like he didn't even want to smell me.''

It was the fire that seemed to hold Seth's attention now, but he held fast to Mariah's hand, as if it grounded him, kept him safe.

''He stepped on a mine and went up like a firecracker.'' His low, quiet voice echoed remembered astonishment. ''Right there in front of me. Knocked me flat, and when I sat up…there he stood.''

''St-stood?''

''Stood. He didn't even look like—'' Not like Hughy. Nothing like Hughy. *There was nothing human about the specter except the eyes.* ''He looked like something that's been left on the grill too long.'' Seth closed his eyes. His own flippancy stabbed him in the gut like an attack of appendicitis. Hughy wouldn't have approved.

His eyesight blurred, and he blinked furiously, trying to focus on the fire. *Just tell her straight out if you're so damned determined to spill your guts.*

''He screamed—more like an animal than a man. I called out to him, but I was…it was like I was paralyzed.'' Mouth dry, throat stinging, he swallowed and plunged into the worst of it—the darkest part of the nightmare. ''He…he begged me to shoot him. 'For God's sake, Cantrell, shoot me!' All I remember saying is 'Damn, damn, damn.' I shouldered my rifle. My best friend was in my sights. And then I heard a shot.''

''Oh, Seth.''

God, she was still there. He turned at the sound of her voice and wondered why she hadn't bolted. ''It wasn't me,'' he told her. ''Thank God, it wasn't me.'' She lifted her free hand to touch his face, but he pushed it down, then held on to it. ''I don't know why I didn't see it coming. It should have been me.''

"No, Seth. It wasn't your fault."

Her eyes were full of tears, but he knew the tears were for him, not Hughy. She hadn't seen him. She hadn't smelled his charred flesh, or heard the death rattle in his throat. She had no idea what the tattered uniform and the charred skin had left exposed.

"I mean, I should have been the one to shoot him, not some damn VC sniper. I could have done it quick and clean, just like I did for the bear the other day. Hughy wouldn't have felt another second of pain. But there was another shot, then another, and Hughy—" What he remembered was unspeakable. He shook his head, hoping to dislodge the image. "I came to my senses and blasted that bastard out of his tree."

Mariah tried hard to blink back her tears. Seth's tears shimmered in his eyes, but they wouldn't fall. "And your friend?" she asked.

"It should be quick and clean, Hughy always said. But when it came his turn, he wouldn't go down easy." It had been hard to touch him. There had been no place on his body that wasn't raw. "My friend Hughy died in my arms."

He wouldn't allow *her* to touch *him*, either, but he continued to hold her hands as if they were his lifeline. "Then you did all that a friend could do, Seth."

"What good did it do?" he demanded. "Any way you look at it, I was dealing in death. Just like the grizzly. Death was the best I had to offer him."

"Seth." What could she say to this man? He needed forgiveness, absolution, and he held her away from him even as he looked to her for those things. "You need balance in your life. If you cut yourself off from people because you're afraid—"

"I'm not afraid. I'm realistic."

"Then listen to me. When I first came up here, I didn't know what I was going to do about the baby. I knew what I wanted to do, but I knew I'd be blowing my shot at the ski team, letting a bunch of people down, and I wasn't sure I could make that decision." She tugged against his grip. "No," she whispered. "Let me touch you. Let me tell you what you've done for me."

"I've done nothing," he said, but he released her hands and let her put them on his unworthy face. He closed his eyes and savored her cool, clean touch.

She slipped her arms around him and laid her head against his chest. Neither of them spoke. She heard his heartbeat quicken, and she imagined that his eyes were still closed, and that unspoken questions were running riot in his head, as they were in hers.

"I can do it now, Seth," she told him finally. One question was at last resolved. "I know I can, and I feel good about it. You said I had to do what was right for *me*, and that's what I'm going to do."

"You're going to have the baby."

He sounded almost afraid to say it, but that was okay. *She* wasn't afraid. She rubbed her cheek against his shirt. "Yes."

"And you're going to let me help you, right?" She leaned back to look up at him questioningly. Immediately he pulled her into his arms, pressing her head back where she'd first put it—where he wanted it—leaning against him. "Any way at all, Mariah. Let me pay the bills. Let me…let me take those classes with you and be with you when—"

The helicopter was a rude interruption, and Seth realized that for the first time he hadn't picked up the sound when it was too faint to be heard by anyone but a paranoid vet or a German shepherd. The damn thing had sneaked right up on him.

Reluctantly they drew apart.

Seth held Mariah at arm's length and plumbed her eyes for assurance. "I'll have to go with him, but I want you here when I get back, okay?"

She smiled. "Where would I go?"

"I don't know. Nowhere, I guess. I just—" He floundered and finally rose from the seat. Mariah followed, still smiling. "I want you here. That's what I'm saying."

"Okay."

"We'll work this out. You be thinking—" The volume of the thumping blades increased overhead. Seth raised his voice. "You be thinking about ways…I want you to tell me what you want me to do, and be honest, okay?"

"Okay."

He edged toward the door, grabbing his jacket off the chair on his way. "Because it's no trouble," he insisted, keeping his eyes on her as he speared one arm into a sleeve. "Whatever you need. Whatever I can do. You think about it."

"I will."

"We'll make plans." Blindly he donned a glove. "You and me. Together."

The noise drowned out her voice, but he read her lips. "I understand."

"So I'll see you in a little while," he shouted as he pulled on the second glove.

She closed the distance between them in two short steps, put her hand behind his neck and brought his head down for a kiss. He let it be her gift, and when she whispered, "See you in a little while," he flashed her a bright, unguarded smile.

Chapter Nine

Seth's emotions had played havoc with his visceral moorings, and the *whap whap whap* of the chopper blades had his gut quivering like gelatin in a bowl. He gripped his knees and leaned into the job of scouting for some trace of the two men who used assault weapons and aliases in territory where there shouldn't have been much use for either. As intriguing as their motives might be, Seth had to keep prodding himself to take this search seriously. Forget about everything else for now, he told himself. Everything but the reason you're skimming over the tops of these spruce trees.

He sat back and cast a furtive glance at the profile of pilot, Charlie Day, then Howard Polanski, the game warden. Two pairs of aviator glasses betrayed no sign of disgust. Surely, Seth reasoned, there was weakness and embarrassment written all over his face. Seth almost expected to hear Polanski say, *You been telling your war*

*stories. Must be a sympathetic female hiding out at the
station, huh? What's her name? She got a friend?*

She's got me, Seth thought. For whatever that's worth.
It had taken Mariah only a few days to get him to bare
his soul. The shrinks in the VA hospital had been at it
for months before they got anything out of him. Maybe
she was in the wrong line of work.

Hell, what was he thinking? She wasn't working on
him. He was working on her, and had been since that
first night. A man didn't let a woman get to him like that
unless he had a pretty good reason, right? Of course, he
was a little foggy about exactly what his motives were
at this point. She hadn't held out on him, hadn't played
hard to get. She probably had her reasons, too, but she
hadn't asked him for anything. In fact, *he'd* had to plead
with *her* just to think about letting him…

Letting him what? What good could he do her? She
probably didn't need his money, and the idea of taking
childbirth classes and helping her in the delivery room
was pure insanity. Where the hell had that come from,
anyway? All of a sudden he'd had this crazy picture of
the two of them—her shaped like a beach ball with limbs,
and him nervous as hell—the *two* of them trying to have
a baby, for God's sake. Maybe he needed to go back for
a checkup.

"Here's the campsite we checked before." Polanski's
sudden announcement made Seth jump. "You daydream-
ing, Cantrell? This is it, ain't it?"

"Yeah, this is it." *Jeez, relax.*

The three men peered through the helicopter's bubble.
Treetops slid beneath them like a rolling carpet. "You
didn't see any sign of horses or anything?" Polanski
asked.

"No, no horses. There was a lot of stuff there, though. You'd think they had to pack it in."

"And AR-15s, you say?"

"Yeah, which could easily match up with the .223 caliber slug I took out of that bear. I'd say they took those potshots at the bighorns with a long-action hunting rifle, probably a .338, so they're pretty well armed."

"And loaded for bear or anything else that comes along." Polanski pulled his pile-lined cap off and ran his fingers through hair that reminded Seth of dirty dishwater. He settled the cap back in place and nodded at Seth. "Nobody could accuse you of not knowing your firearms, Cantrell."

Seth shrugged. "Man's gotta specialize in something."

"So you heard a .338, but all you saw was AR-15s."

"Right."

"And they were on foot."

"That's right."

Polanski stretched his neck to look past the pilot's shoulder. "Some kind of radical rednecks, I s'pose," he muttered.

"What're you talking about, Polanski?" Seth chuckled as he watched a rocky meadow slide beneath them. "You're the biggest redneck I know."

"Yeah, but I'm not one of these card-carryin' *radical* rednecks. I don't have any off-the-wall ideas about—"

"You don't have too many ideas, period." Charlie's unexpected dig made Seth laugh and Polanski scowl. With that kind of encouragement Charlie couldn't help elaborating. "You don't even have a library card."

"Who needs one? I don't have to do much reading to keep up my end of a conversation with you, Charlie boy." Pleased with his comeback, Polanski scanned the ridge that loomed dead ahead. "Damn, I hate it when we get these jokers up here."

"Pilots or poachers?" Seth wondered absently. If he hadn't trusted Charlie's skill, he would have been bracing himself for a collision with the sheer rock face.

"Anybody who's off-the-wall, which we're gonna be in about—hey, don't screw around now, Charlie!"

Charlie veered the aircraft away from the ridge after maneuvering a hair-raising near-miss. He and Seth shared another laugh as the helicopter gave their stomachs a quick bounce before sailing over the crest.

"Yeah, funny," Polanski grumbled. "I get a real bang out of you army vets and your sense of humor."

"So it's the poachers you hate," Seth concluded, still sharing a grin with Charlie.

"*These* poachers," Polanski said. "These survivalists, or whatever they're calling themselves. We'll find out when we catch up to them. You know damn well we're gonna end up bringing in a bunch of investigators, going to court for weeks on end, filing reports. Hell, just give me a plain ol' poacher any day. Flash of the badge scares the pants off him. Impound his pickup and his hunting rifle, you teach him a good lesson. That's what this job is s'posed to be all about."

"The job's about sparing these last little corners of wilderness from idiots of every description," Seth claimed.

"You're such a damn purist, Cantrell."

"So where to now, gentlemen?" Charlie put in.

"Take us down to Point 8541." Crawford's Mountain, Seth added silently. "That's where we…that's where we met up."

Through the cabin window Mariah watched the helicopter disappear from sight. Seth would be back in a little while. He'd promised. How little? she wondered. They had been talking about important things—really, honestly talking—and suddenly there was this stupid helicopter. He hadn't even had his breakfast. She hadn't, either, but she wasn't hungry.

In fact, she was restless. Seth was out searching for two men he considered to be dangerous. It had gone without saying that she should bolt the door and stay out of sight, but the cabin had three blind sides, and she didn't like the idea that somebody might sneak up on her. The lookout tower would afford her a better view, and when the helicopter returned, she figured she could hide behind the desk just in case Seth brought anyone up there. She would listen hard for that helicopter, and she'd hear it, just the way Seth usually did, before they could spot her in the tower. In the meantime, if she saw anything suspicious, she knew how to use the radio.

The back room yielded a couple of strips of beef jerky, which she pocketed for lunch, and Seth's revolver. He had been talking, thinking about other things—she smiled, remembering the endearing way he'd expressed his concerns—and all of a sudden he'd had to deal with that helicopter. Apparently he hadn't thought about taking a weapon. But she figured the men in the helicopter were armed, and Seth probably didn't expect to find much. If those poachers had any brains at all, she told herself, they would be long gone by now.

She would still feel more secure in the tower.

Carrying the revolver in one hand and her gloves under her arm, she secured the cabin door. What had begun as a bright blue morning was turning gray, which was typical of the ever-changing mountain weather. Snow and gravel crunched under her hiking boots as she rounded the corner of the cabin and started to sidestep the dwindling woodpile.

Something came crunching behind her. She froze, but only momentarily, then gripped the pistol and did a quick about-face.

The man who'd been introduced simply as Gordie stood there grinning at her. He had a black stocking cap pulled snugly over his ears. His chin was pimply, cheeks smooth, and brown eyes no more threatening than a friendly dog's. "Mornin', ma'am." His eyes shifted toward the woodpile.

At Mariah's back, the woodpile seemed to spring to life. Torn in two directions, she turned a few more degrees, and her weapon was knocked from her hand. She stepped back, reclaiming her balance as she grabbed her smarting right hand with her left.

Ray McKenzie, the man who'd done all the talking when she and Seth had previously met the pair, pocketed the revolver and seized her arm. "First time I laid eyes on you, I says to myself, I'd like to get to know this woman. What d'ya say we go inside and get acquainted?"

The man's foul breath took shape in the cold and puffed in her face. He, too, wore a black stocking cap. His face was drawn, his facial bones prominent, and his brown eyes were anything but friendly. His assault rifle was slung over his shoulder. Her heart skittered against her ribs, but she swallowed the words she knew would come out sounding screechy and terrified. She glared back at her captor.

"Your man's bound and determined to make an issue outa that ol' griz, ain't he?"

Mariah made a vain attempt to jerk her arm away, then

tried to square her shoulders. "Obviously he knows who did it."

"Self-defense," Ray said with a shrug. "Bear came at us outa nowhere."

"He knows you'll say that."

"Who am I gonna say it to? He ain't never gonna catch me." His eyes narrowed as his mouth stretched in a slow grin. "'Less I decide it might be fun to see the look on his face when I got his woman's pants down."

"C'mon," Gordie grumbled, shuffling his feet impatiently in the gravel. "You said we needed supplies."

"Yeah, well I need somethin' else, kid." Gordie stepped back as Ray started around the corner, pushing Mariah ahead of him. "We're gonna get everything we need right here."

"That helicopter will be back any time," Mariah warned as she dragged her feet. "Why don't you just take what you need from the cabin and go? Otherwise—" she stopped at the door and tried once again to jerk away from Ray's hold on her "—otherwise you'll have more trouble than you can handle."

"You don't say." He reached behind her to open the door. "Haven't seen the ranger yet could find me 'less I wanted to be found. Like to let 'em play a little cat and mouse once in a while."

He gave Mariah a shove and smiled when she stumbled over the threshold. She caught her balance, and he followed her inside. She could tell that he wanted her to try something, that he was waiting for her to make a move.

"The cat starts chasin' its own tail," he continued, gesturing with two fingers. "And then the mouse just slips into a hole and disappears."

Mariah wasn't responding the way he wanted. In fact,

she wasn't responding at all. She was just staring at him. Ray gripped her shoulder. "What kinda games do you like to play, little girl? Do you like a little mousey in the hole?"

Gordie appeared in the doorway. "Listen, we don't have time for any games. Let's just get what we need and get outa here. We don't need to mess with her."

Ray laughed. "Maybe *you* don't need to mess with her. What did you do, bypass puberty, boy? Swear to God, you're like some kinda robot."

Gordie stepped inside, eyeing Mariah as he moved carefully around Ray. "How much trouble is he gonna go to over a bear and a few supplies? Huh?" He lifted a hand toward Mariah. "You do his woman, we're gonna be up to our necks in trouble."

"You got nothin' to worry about, boy. He's just a ranger. He comes back, I'll take care of him."

"It's no good, you messin' with women like this," Gordie insisted, flopping his arms against his sides. "Sooner or later, you're gonna bring the law down on us."

"Nobody's ever gonna catch us up here."

"You're sure as hell givin' 'em plenty of reason to try."

Ray dismissed the argument with a sweep of his hand. "See what you can find to pack some supplies in. I'm gettin' sick of venison and rabbit. Over there." He pointed to the hiker's pack leaning against the stone fireplace. "Start with that." He turned to Mariah. "Get over on that bed."

Gordie glanced at Mariah, and she thought she detected a hint of an apology in his face before he turned, snatched up the backpack and headed for the corner of the cabin where the stove stood.

"There's food in the back room," Mariah said, ignoring Ray's command. "Take whatever you need and don't let this go any further." She stared evenly at Ray. "The helicopter could return any time, and then you'll be outnumbered. Why not just go?"

He stared at her with hungry eyes, and she was reminded of his reference to himself as a rodent when he added a feral smile. "Yeah. Why not?"

Gordie stuck his head back into the room. "He's got a couple of nice rifles here—a heavy-duty centerfire and a .22. You want 'em?"

"I don't want to leave 'em with him. See any rope back there?"

Gordie stood for a moment, hard anger in his eyes. Then he took a deep breath and sighed, defeated. "Yeah. How much do you want?"

"Four feet."

Mariah willed the younger man to look at her, see her, know that his reservations were her only chance. He turned away. In a moment he stood in the doorway again and tossed Ray a length of half-inch rope. "Can't you just get it done so we can get out of here?"

Ray snatched the snaking rope out of the air. "I'm gonna put this leash on her."

"What for?"

"We're takin' her with us."

"Takin' her with us?" Gordie shook his head. "I think you've finally lost it."

"Why not? We take what we want, right? This—" he patted his military-style rifle "—is what gives us the right."

"You said you wouldn't do that again. You said we were gonna keep to ourselves, don't let nobody mess with us and we won't mess with them."

Mariah glanced at Ray, but the pieces that were coming together in her mind made her look away. Again? Do what again? Rape? Or something worse?

"Yeah, well…a man can't go too long without a woman. The minute I seen her, I knew it had been too long for me. This isn't your concern, anyway. It's mine. I'll take care of her. You just load up some grub. We oughta be able to carry some ammo, too, with the little lady's help."

Gordie headed for the back room, mumbling obscenities. Cans and boxes were slammed around. "You want his rifles, then?" he called out.

"Clean him out. Might inconvenience him a little. 'Course, he's got a delivery service, but I think Uncle's nephew's got a little secret." Ray secured Mariah's hands in front of her with a couple of half hitches. "I don't expect his bosses know she's up here," he told the man in the back room, then smiled knowingly at Mariah. "Am I right, little lady? The Forest Service doesn't know what Uncle's nephew keeps in his pantry."

Gordie dropped the loaded backpack on the table. "Sometimes the wives stay with these guys if they're seasonal."

"Whose stuff is back there?" Ray asked.

"How the hell do I know?" Gordie went back for the rifles and a canvas sack he'd also filled, adding when he returned, "Pair of men's boots, couple pairs of jeans."

"His?"

"They wouldn't fit her."

Ray surveyed the room. The box under the bed caught his eye, and he moved toward it, tugging Mariah after him with the rope. He rifled through Seth's clothing and came up grinning. "This one's no wife. Am I right, darlin'? There's no woman living here."

Her mouth was dry with fear. She didn't know what difference any of this might make to them. "I...we're friends. I do a lot of hiking, mountain climbing. I just stopped in."

"Stopped in?" Ray laughed. "I don't know what kind of setup you've got here, but I figure you oughta stop in at my place, too."

"C'mon, now, don't take her up to the camp," Gordie pleaded.

"Why the hell not?"

"Can't you just do her and get it over with?"

"What difference does it make?" Ray waited for Mariah to look up at him so she wouldn't mistake his meaning. He liked a scared woman best. "She's seen us now."

Gordie shouldered the .22. "She's just gonna be trouble, that's all."

"Trouble I can handle." Ray reached for the backpack. "Hell." He pulled Mariah closer and began untying her hands. "I don't have to carry this, do I? Got myself a pack horse."

"It's pretty heavy for a woman," Gordie said. But he'd given up. Ray was going to play his games. He helped Mariah with the shoulder straps, and Ray tied her hands again.

"I dropped my gloves outside," she said, trying not to sound desperate. If Seth came back right now, they might kill him. If he didn't, God! These two maniacs were taking her with them. She blinked back tears. "Can't I get my gloves?"

Ray took the canvas sack. "We don't have time to be lookin' for gloves. It ain't that cold out, not yet."

Seth had watched the helicopter take off, then headed for the cabin. Inexplicably, he had a bad feeling about the quiet when he pushed the door open.

"Mariah?"

No answer. He felt a dizzying rush of alarm as he stalked past the box of personal items that should have been under the bed, past the table he'd come to expect to be set for a meal this time of day and through the door to the back room. He found a mess. Rifles—gone. Pistol—gone. Ammunition and much of his food supply—also gone. He spun on his heel, the sound of her name pounding in his brain as he headed outside. One blue glove lay next to the woodpile, another a couple of feet away. He swept them up and saw one clear boot print, too large to be Mariah's, too small to be his. The spot was heavily tracked, but that one print was clear.

Seth took off like a runner out of the starting blocks, never quite straightening from a crouch as he scrambled up the hill toward the tower. Fear for Mariah pushed aside his combat instincts, and it didn't occur to him to suspect a trap until he bounded up the stairs to the catwalk and threw open the door to the observation deck. Somebody could have been waiting to blindside him, and he would have flown into the snare. But no one was there, and his own panting terror was deafening.

He paced the glass-sided square like an animal in a shipping crate. Gray clouds loomed low in the sky. He had about two hours of daylight left. He could call Charlie back and get a helicopter search going. He started for the radio, but a picture took shape in his mind that made him hesitate. Ray McKenzie and his sidekick, outfitted in their toy action figure costumes and even better armed than they had been before, were holding Mariah. They had their hands on her. Their rifle barrels hovered inches from her head. A chopper would just make them edgy.

They'd find a place to hole up, which wouldn't be so bad, except that they would be holing up with Mariah. After dark the helicopter would have to use spotlights. Hunted men, backed into a corner, holding a woman. Mariah had a better chance of staying alive if Seth tracked them on his own.

But he needed some insurance. If he slipped, if they got him somehow, they could make off with her, and who would know? He decided to put in the call. He would have to trust Charlie Day.

"Yes, sir, mountain man," Charlie's voice answered. "Miss us already?"

"Our rabbits have been here, Charlie. They raided my carrot patch up here. Got that?"

"Affirmative, Cantrell. Returning to—"

"No, stay on course. It's almost dark. I'm like an owl at night, buddy. I'm going rabbit hunting."

"What do you need?"

A few more hours of daylight. "I want you back here at first light. Look for smoke."

"What if I don't see any?"

"Then you organize a manhunt. There's a good chance they're holding a hostage. Woman named Mariah Crawford."

"What do you mean? How do you—"

"Don't ask too many questions. I, uh…I know this woman, okay? Just give me twelve hours, Charlie. No feds for twelve hours. I'm the only one who's in any position to find anything before morning, anyway. If there's a bird in the air, rabbits get nervous. I think I can get to them without spooking them." Seth drew a deep breath. Contingency plan, he reminded himself. Insurance. "If there's no signal come morning, you get some people to go after her. Good people. You hear me?"

"Roger. You're talking specialists."

"I'm counting on you, Charlie. Leave Polanski out of it and give me 'til morning."

Charlie's sign-off left a terrible silence. Seth was alone in this now, at least until daybreak, and he could only hope he was calling the right shots. He was going after her on his own. There wasn't a man in the whole state of Montana who was better prepared for the mission. Seek and destroy. Track down and eliminate. Take the enemy by surprise. But the objective was not killing, which he knew he could accomplish with skilled ease. The mission was Mariah.

Seth dressed and armed himself. It amused him to think that the two who had taken Mariah had also taken his firearms. No Guns, No Glory was undoubtedly their motto. He removed the custom-made specialty knife from its sheath. It fit his grip and his style. In his hand the finely honed blade would be deadlier in the silence of the night than the entire arsenal at McKenzie's disposal.

The only wild card in Seth's hand was his fear for Mariah's safety. He couldn't let himself think about what they might have done to her already. Those thoughts would bring him perilously close to letting emotion control him. He needed the cold nerve he'd once valued, the steely attitude he had tempered in the furnace of war. If he thought about how much he had to lose on this mission, he was apt to make a fatal mistake.

McKenzie had made some attempt to cover the trail, but Seth had no trouble picking it up. The two men were carrying extra rifles and supplies and dragging a reluctant woman along. Seth knew he would catch up with them no matter what kind of a head start they had on him. When he did, he was going to have trouble resisting the urge to rush them. It was important to pick his time and his spot. Then the show would be all his.

Mariah's tow rope had been removed, but not before it had rubbed the skin of her wrists raw. The backpack full of stolen supplies weighed heavily on her shoulders. Stuffed into her jacket pockets, her fingers were numb with cold, but she didn't complain. Night had fallen, and Gordie, who was behind her, had already spoken of stopping to make camp. The prospect scared her as much as the fact that her body increasingly threatened to give in to exhaustion. If she dropped, they might leave her where she lay, or *use* her, then leave her. If they stopped, she was afraid she would become the entertainment for the night. As long as she kept moving, she told herself she was okay.

Winter's night brightness was trapped between the snow on the ground and the promise of more snow overhead. Trees at this elevation were scrubby and sparse. There was no wind, and nothing stirred but the brush slapping against the hikers' pants. Only Mariah breathed heavily enough to be heard.

Ray broke their trail through the knee-high brush. He was tireless, despite the rifle and the canvas pack he carried. "We'll go as far as Skunk Wallow tonight," he announced over his shoulder. "They'll be searching bright and early, and I wanna make sure we've got overhead cover."

"She won't hold out for another two hours," Gordie said. "We gotta take a break or we'll be carrying her."

"Five minutes," Ray decided, coming to an abrupt halt. He grabbed Mariah by the shoulders and backed her up to a rock. "Sit here," he commanded. "Take a load off."

The two men squatted on either side of the rock, and Gordie pulled a round can of smokeless tobacco out of his back pocket. He offered Ray the first dip, along with a quiet suggestion as he watched the older man help himself to a pinch of the snuff. "I think we oughta just let her go."

"We're keepin' her with us for a while." Ray tucked the tobacco in his lower lip. Gordie wasn't hard enough, not yet. He had to be told a fairy tale now and again. "Hey, she's not makin' no fuss. Women stop complaining sooner or later, and then they just go along. We're gonna have to head for new territory anyway, and…well, we got her now. We might as well make use of her."

Mariah tried to shut the whole thing out. She needed this rest. That was all she wanted to think about.

"We're gonna end up with the same problem we had the last time you had to have yourself a woman."

She didn't know if she cared what problem they'd had.

"Nobody ever found her," Ray pointed out. "Big manhunt, all them dogs and helicopters, and they never turned up nothin'."

"Yeah, but that ranger's seen us. And she's gotta be his woman. He'll be huntin' us 'til—"

"Let him hunt us." Ray's grin was slow and sinister. "'Til we catch him."

Catch Seth? Mariah thought. She'd like to see them try.

"You said we didn't need anybody else," Gordie pouted. "No neighbors, tax collectors, no bankers. Us against the world—that's what you said—and we don't need none of their interference. These—" he reached over his shoulder and grabbed a rifle barrel "—are for self-defense."

"We got a right to defend ourselves." It was Ray's

motto. Not too many people were willing to mess with a man holding an AR-15.

"I agree. But we got no right to kidnap people."

"The woman was there for the taking."

"I say you're pushing your luck."

Mariah cleared her throat, but her attempt to make herself heard started out raspy anyway. "How...how far is it to this Skunk Wallow."

"Not too far." Ray grinned up at her. "Anxious?"

"Skunk Wallow is what we call one of our campsites, where we got a cache, sort of like a hunter's blind," Gordie explained. He couldn't help feeling sorry for the woman. She was pretty, and she'd toughed it out like a trooper so far.

"You guys made it kinda inconvenient for us when you found Duck Noose camp." Ray turned his head and spat into the snow. "Took a lotta work to relocate that one."

"Well, I told you we was gettin' too close to that ranger station," Gordie reminded Ray. Then he turned back to Mariah. "Anyways, we move around a lot, but we do like the Indians do. We got caches of supplies here and there, so we never have to depend on one spot."

"Is this the way you live?" she asked. Not that she cared, but she didn't want to move yet. "You just stay up here all the time?"

"Like he says, we move around a lot. Free and independent," Ray boasted. "We don't owe nobody nothin'."

"Obviously, you're very good at what you do. Why don't you just leave me here and go on your way? You could be miles away from here by the time they find me, and as long as you haven't done me any harm, I don't see any reason to—"

"I got a use for you, little lady. We'll be on our way, but you're comin' along—" Ray chortled "—just for the ride, you might say."

Mariah looked to Gordie for support, but he was hunched over, staring at the ground.

"Let's get movin'," Ray said, straightening his wiry frame. "I wanna be in the hole down at Skunk Wallow come mornin'." His turn of phrase struck him funny, and he punched Gordie's shoulder. "In the hole, I says."

Ray was the only one who laughed.

Chapter Ten

Cold, sickening fear lay like a lump in the pit of Seth's stomach. He crouched behind a tree, breathed without making a sound and slipped his gloves off in absolute silence, but inside his head Mariah's name echoed so loudly he could hardly think. He'd found the two men, but Mariah wasn't anywhere to be seen. If they had done any harm to her, they were dead men. He would pick his time, pick his spot and end their miserable lives. He began to reconstruct the layers of anger he'd spent years tearing down, building on that hard lump of fear as the core. He was looking at men who were already dead in his mind, their blood turning the white snow red.

In the near-light of early morning, Gordie watched Ray pace. It was always like this when a woman came into the picture. The old man always had to work himself into a frenzy. It was going to be a long day and Gordie dreaded it. He wished he could just take a hike and come back when it was over. Ray couldn't just "do her and get it over with." He had to scare the woman half out of her wits, get her to cry and beg for mercy. So far this one wasn't cooperating.

Gordie had learned that sex was a disgusting, demeaning proposition for both parties, and he wanted no part of it. He wished he could distract Ray from going through the whole damn charade again, but he'd gotten himself started on it now, and there would be no stopping him until he'd done her his way.

Gordie took a seat on a rock. "When are we leavin' here?" he asked disinterestedly. He knew it wouldn't be soon enough.

Carrying his rifle on his shoulder like a sentry, Ray strode toward Gordie. "Maybe not 'til tonight. If they send choppers up right away, we'll have to stay outa sight." He turned on his heel and paced in the other direction, moving nervously, like a man driven to some invisible brink. "'Sides, I got somethin' goin' here."

"It's a demon." Gordie's tone was hopeless. "You got a demon eatin' on your insides."

"Demon, hell!" Ray whirled as if to knock the accusation down physically. "I'm a man. I'm just like any other man."

"Yeah, I know."

"Ain't nobody gonna tell me how to run my life."

"Nobody's tryin'."

"Not a twit like you, anyway." Ray bent toward Gordie and poked a finger in his face. "You ain't normal, boy. I don't even think your gun's got a barrel on it."

Gordie had heard all this before, and he wasn't going to let it bother him. He sort of hoped the woman couldn't hear it, though. For some reason, he didn't want her thinking he was like Ray.

* * *

Mariah heard nothing. She saw nothing; she felt nothing but the cold. The smell of earth was all around her in the small dark place where she sat hugging her knees. Her hands were tied, but not her feet. She could taste gun oil on the rag Ray had tied over her mouth, and she tried not to swallow. She imagined herself choking to death on her own vomit. Her fingers and toes were numb, but she could move them. She told herself over and over that Seth would come. He would find her. He would not let that man touch her again. And the baby would be fine. The baby was safe inside her, and it would be fine. The baby would be fine, would be fine, would be fine.

Seth had gauged Ray's pacing as he positioned himself to strike. The sky was lightening. He crouched, gripping his knife, as he watched the man turn and take the first of the six steps that were his pattern.

"Gonna have to travel light," Ray mumbled.

Two, three.

"Make sure the body won't be found."

Four, you murdering bastard. Five.

"No other way to—"

Seth sprang, lifting Gordie from the rock like a sack of meal. He could feel the young man's scrawny throat yield to the point of his knife, but Seth's eyes—the terrible eyes of the walking dead—were on Ray. "I'll bleed him like a pig before I butcher you, McKenzie," he called. "Where is she? Where'd you put her body?"

Ray grabbed for his rifle.

"Yeah, shoot us both, you bastard. I swear to God, I won't go down without taking you with me."

"She ain't dead," Gordie choked out.

Ray bolted heading for higher ground, but Gordie's words had claimed every shred of Seth's attention. Not dead? He turned the blade away from the man's throat so that only the point was a threat to him. "Where is she?"

"I'll show you."

"No tricks, kid," Seth warned. He struggled to keep up a hard front, but for a moment he'd thought she was dead, and his own heart had turned to stone. Gordie's three words had turned winter to spring. Now Seth's heart beat wildly, and though he lived again, he could hardly breathe.

"No tricks." Gordie lifted his hand and pointed through the trees. Seth held the knife a hair's breadth from the younger man's throat as they moved together. At the edge of a small clearing, Seth's rifles stood against a tree, along with Mariah's backpack and a canvas pack.

Gordie continued to point, and Seth could feel the trembling in the young man's body. He knew he'd drawn blood. He could feel it dribbling on his hand. "Where?" he demanded.

"Let me show you."

It looked like a deadfall at the edge of the clearing. Seth remembered the setup at the camp he'd discovered—the hunter's blind, the cache of supplies and ammunition. They'd put her in a hole! He pushed Gordie aside and lunged toward the spot, calling her name.

Seth heard the shot and felt the streak of white heat against his temple almost simultaneously. The jolt knocked him off his feet and painted splotches of black on the dawning day. He dug his fingers into the layers of snow and dry pine needles, struggling to push himself up. His head felt as though it were cracking open, like an egg. The edge of his hand brushed against the handle of his knife, and he grabbed it, stabbed it into the ground and broke the tip of the blade. He was successful with the second stab. He gripped the handle and pulled himself a few inches closer to the hole he believed—he *knew*—contained Mariah.

"Stay down," Gordie pleaded. "Let him think he got you."

Seth ignored the voice as he tried to sort the branches that covered the blind from his brain's own inky blind spots. "Stay there, Mariah," he called. "Don't move, honey."

Somewhere in the black periphery Seth heard a breech bolt slide and click back into place. He turned his head, knowing that among the black spots and the strange red sparks, he would be looking down the barrel of his own rifle.

Please, God. Let me see her first.

Gordie was aiming at the ledge just beyond the tree-tops. Seth turned his head again, just in time to get a faceful of needles and dirt scattered by another poorly aimed shot.

"Drop it, Dad," Gordie whispered. "Please."

Seth managed to focus on the man on the ridge just as Gordie fired. Quick and clean. Ray fell, as if in slow motion, his rifle flying end over end in one direction as he jackknifed and tumbled straight down in another.

"Crazy ol' man," Gordie screamed as he threw Seth's rifle aside. "You never could shoot worth a damn."

"Mariah," Seth shouted. He pushed himself away from the ground on unsteady arms. "Why doesn't she answer me? Is she hurt? Mariah!"

"She's got a gag in her mouth," Gordie answered flatly. "She's all right."

Seth struggled to his feet. Blood trickled into his right eye. "Get a fire going, will you, Gordie? She's gotta be—'' he stumbled and went back down on one knee ''—frozen stiff. Damn, I can't see straight.''

"I'll get her out," Gordie offered dazedly.

But Mariah's head appeared amid the branches like a ground squirrel popping up for some morning sunlight. Seth tried to blink back the encroaching blackness for a glimpse of her wild hair and green eyes. Her face was scratched, and her mouth was covered with a filthy rag, but the sight of her made his heart swell.

"Thank God," he whispered.

Mariah made the first move after Gordie removed the gag. She didn't wait for him to untie her hands, but ran to Seth with tethered arms outstretched. "Seth, what happened? Who shot—you're hurt."

"I'm okay. McKenzie was up on the ridge. He took a couple of shots at me before the kid nailed him." He closed his hands over the ropes as she knelt beside him. "Gordie, please find something to cut these with. I broke my—" He closed his eyes and touched his lips to her thumbs, muttering words of prayer and praise.

"Seth, your head."

"It's just a scratch." He took the knife Gordie handed him and went to work on the bonds around her wrists, but his hands didn't seem to belong to him, and his vision was cloudy.

"Let me do it."

With an effort, Seth turned his head toward the voice. He could make out the eyes—brown and full of tears. A kid's eyes. A kid who'd just done a man's job. *The kid nailed him* had been a bad choice of words. "He was your father?" Gordie stared and nodded. "Why'd you do it?"

"There was no other way to make him stop." Gordie held out his hand. "I won't hurt her. I swear."

Seth relinquished the knife. "Getting a little dizzy," he admitted. "I've gotta trust you, kid. She needs a fire. Her hands...so damn cold."

Gordie did as Seth asked. He wanted to put off his other responsibility as long as possible. Once he had the fire going, he squatted close to it and watched Mariah cradle Seth's unconscious head in her lap. He'd seen the way his father touched women, and the way they tried to fight him off. Gordie had never wanted any part of it. As far back as he could remember, back to the mother who had finally run away, he had never seen a man treat a woman's hands as gently as Seth just had. And he'd never seen a woman look at a man that way. Maybe if...sometime if a woman would touch him that way...maybe he wouldn't mind so much.

Mariah wiped away her tears with the heel of her hand and looked up at him. "It's not bleeding so much now. It doesn't look too bad, does it, Gordie?"

"No, it don't look too bad." In the distance he heard a helicopter. He wasn't so dumb. He knew what the smoke was for. "I better go see to my dad," he said, resigning himself to it with a long, hollow sigh.

"I don't think you want to see him now."

"I can't just leave him there." He stood and seemed to try to get his bearings.

"Gordie, if you run, they'll catch up to you."

Gordie looked down at Seth and the woman who obviously loved him. "I ain't runnin' no more."

It seemed rude to be shaking a man who'd found a good place to hibernate. Seth felt the intrusion and distantly heard the strange female voice saying, "That's right, Mr. Cantrell. Open your eyes. Come on, you can do it."

Sure, he could do it. He could open his eyes anytime, but gradually. A little at a time. There was whiteness, brightness, wire-rimmed glasses and gray hair. He slammed his eyelids down. The dark cave was a hell of a lot more soothing than all that light, and he had a killer of a hangover. He tried to tell the wire rims to get lost, but all he could manage was a grunt.

"No you don't, Mr. Cantrell. You've been out long enough. Come on, now, work at it. Come on back."

He admitted another slit of light. Starched white pocket over an ample breast. Black name tag, white letters, Lydia Gillette, R.N. What was R.N.? Rude nurse?

"Where's the john?" Seth grumbled.

"Aha! A complete sentence. You've returned to the land of the living."

"Yeah. Here I am." He closed his eyes again, figuring he could find out where *here* was in a minute. First things first. First the irritating light, then the voice of some female comic, then the urge he wasn't even sure he could control. "So answer my question."

"That's all being taken care of for you, Mr. Cantrell. You don't really need a toilet. You only think you do because—"

"The hell, you say." His eyes were open now, but all he could tell was that, wherever he was, it was brighter than blazes. And his right ear was ringing to beat hell. "I'm thirty-seven years old, lady. I know when it's time to head for the john."

"Because of the catheter, which permits you to void without—" he managed to raise himself up on one elbow, but Nurse Gillette pushed him back against the pillow without missing a beat "—any effort on your part.

It's the tube putting pressure on your bladder that makes you feel—''

''Is this a hospital?''

She laughed, and he saw that her face wasn't so unpleasant after all. ''Thirty-seven years old, and he has to ask. I'll get the doctor, Mr. Cantrell.''

Seth watched the stout lady march out the door, her crepe soles squeaking as she did a forty-five-degree turn in the hallway. Then he took inventory of his situation. There was a needle stuck in the back of his hand and held in place with tape, and his arm was strapped to a board. The clear tubing led to a bottle of glucose and water. He looked down at the white sheet that covered him, then craned his neck to peek over the side of the bed. There was a plastic bag, filled with— He dropped back against the pillow. Damn, what a place to stick a tube.

Nurse Gillette returned with another woman—a pretty brunette wearing a white coat. Seth hoped she wouldn't notice that damn bag.

''Mr. Cantrell, I'm Dr. Ressler. It's really good to see the color of your eyes this morning.''

''Manure brown.''

''Yes, I imagine that's just about how you feel.'' She smiled and turned to the nurse. ''Would you call the man who came in with him?'' She turned back to Seth with another smile. ''Actually, I knew. I've had a peek.''

''Oh, yeah?'' He lifted the arm that was strapped to the board. ''Well, just how long have I been lying here while you guys took your peeks and stuck me with things?''

''About forty hours since they brought you in. Bear with me a minute, please.'' She shone a light in his eyes, asked him to follow it, then clicked it off. ''Do you remember what happened to you?'' Dr. Ressler asked as she straightened and looked down her pretty nose at him.

His head was pounding. He touched his right temple gingerly and found a bandage. ''Gunshot wound?'' The doctor nodded. He thought back to a chopper engine roaring in his ears. ''I remember puking my guts out.''

''You've had a severe concussion, and that's par for the course. The helicopter pilot has been here since they brought you in.''

''So where am I?''

''Columbus Hospital. Great Falls. They brought you both here.''

''Both?''

Charlie Day rapped on the open door and grinned. ''I was beginning to wonder if you were gonna sleep for twenty years, Cantrell.''

''Charlie.''

Dr. Ressler backed away and let Charlie take her place at Seth's bedside. ''We know a whole lot more about those two now, and I can fill you in if you want,'' Charlie offered. ''You should've heard Polanski quiz me after you radioed the helicopter. I kept him out of it, like you said, and was he burned.''

''I don't—'' Seth looked from one face to the other. *Two. Those two. They brought you both here.* ''Things are coming back to me kinda like thick, slow-pouring syrup.'' He touched the bandage again. ''You're a long way from home, aren't you, Charlie?''

''They checked all your records, where it says *In case of emergency, please notify.* You never filled in that blank, Cantrell. So I didn't know if you wanted us to track somebody down, and Mariah didn't, either.''

Mariah. The name hit Seth's consciousness like a

thunderbolt, and he repeated it, recalling her eyes, her face, her hands. "Where is she?"

"She's here," Dr. Ressler reported. "She's on another floor. Her doctor ordered bed rest, but she wouldn't co-operate until they brought her down here in a wheelchair to see you. Since then she's been—"

"Take these tubes out," Seth ordered.

The doctor gave his immobilized arm a patronizing pat. "Now that you've regained consciousness, the catheter will be removed, but you still need the continuous fluid because—"

"The whole works. Take it out now. I've gotta—" He glanced down at his chest and grabbed a handful of blue-and-white cotton fabric. "What the hell is this?"

"It's a johnny coat, Mr. Cantrell. A hospital gown."

He looked to a man for help. "Find my pants, Charlie. I've gotta see her."

"I don't know, buddy. Maybe you'd better wait—"

Seth gripped the metal railings and pulled himself up. "Forget the pants, then. Why does she need bed rest? What did McKenzie do to her, huh? Did he hurt her?" He jerked on one railing and managed to knock it down. It took all three people to restrain him, and even then, if he hadn't started to black out, he thought he might have made it. He hung his head for a moment, trying to let it clear, then looked up at Charlie. "Did he hurt her?"

"I don't know what he did. All I know is his real name was Morton, he's dead, and the son's in custody. Mariah gave a report—"

Seth turned to Dr. Ressler. "How is she?"

"Her condition is stable."

"Stable. What does that mean?"

"It means she's—"

"Look, I don't need any of this crap." Seth ripped the

tape off his hand and pulled out the IV needle. "I need to see Mariah. I need to hear her tell me."

The doctor ordered some light food while Nurse Gillette saw to it that all the troublesome tubes were disconnected. Seth figured there were parts of his body that might never function properly again. He agreed to eat because he didn't want to pass out at Mariah's feet, but he insisted on jeans and a shirt. He gave in to the scuffs for his feet because it was quicker, and he let Charlie push him in a wheelchair only as far as the door to Mariah's room.

"I'll catch another ride back," Seth said as he levered himself out of the wheelchair and offered Charlie his hand. "Thanks for looking out for me."

"You wanna fill in those blanks?" Charlie asked. "I could call somebody for you."

"I'll do it myself later. Anyway, there's nothing to report now." He clapped a hand on Charlie's shoulder. "I didn't kick the bucket after all."

"Right." Charlie indicated the closed door with his chin. "I hope everything's okay with her."

"Yeah. Thanks." Seth sucked in a breath and rapped quietly on the door as Charlie pushed the wheelchair down the hall.

The door wasn't quite closed, and no one answered Seth's knock. He glanced around. There was no one to tell him he *couldn't* go in, so he pushed the door open. A broad-shouldered man with thinning hair and reading glasses balanced on the end of his nose dozed in a chair. *Great. Her father.* That was the only thought Seth spared for the man before turning his attention toward the bed.

Mariah was asleep, too. She looked much the way she

had when he'd found her sleeping in his bed—sort of like a child lost in the woods. A far cry from the siren he'd met that first night at Telly's. Well, maybe not such a far cry. Whenever they'd made love, he'd had his siren back. He thought about announcing his presence, but he didn't. He was drawn toward the bed, and his scuffs made no noise as he approached. He eased himself down on the side of the bed and sat, just looking.

There had been no time to hold her, no time for touching and kissing and telling her how glad he was to find her alive. He studied the scratches on her face. They came from hiking at night, of course, but what other damage had been done? Something clawed inside his throat, something scratchy, like the pine needles that had hurt her face. He swallowed, but that only made his throat burn. The whole time he'd been trailing her abductors, he had battled with images that had threatened to render him helpless with rage. Mariah falling on the trail. Mariah's head bashed by the butt of a gun. Some creep touching her, humiliating her, forcing himself on her. Some scum aiming a gun at her back and pulling the trigger.

Emotions. Feelings. God, how they got caught in your throat. And now he was so damn happy just to see a flyaway bit of her hair flutter softly each time she exhaled. He reached for it and smiled when it curled like a baby's hand around his finger. He leaned closer, put his lips a scant inch from her ear and whispered her name.

Her lashes fluttered. Her eyes opened, and she turned her head toward the soft, low voice. He drew back to give her a good look. Her eyes widened. "Seth?" She smiled, a wonderful, shimmery-eyed smile, and grabbed his hand from her cheek, squeezing it tight. "Seth, you're okay?"

"I should be. They tell me I've been sleeping for two days."

"Sleeping? You were unconscious. They let me see you once, and you were just lying there, so—" She put her arms around his neck and let him take her off the pillow and into his arms. "Oh, Seth," she said, and because it sounded so good, and it felt so good to hug him, she repeated it twice more.

"What about you?" he whispered. "Is everything okay?"

"I didn't lose the baby. I hope you're not unhappy about that, because everyone else..." She peered over Seth's shoulder and saw her father sitting bolt upright and waiting for an explanation. "Seth, I think you should meet my father."

He didn't want to let her go.

"Sorry to wake you, Mr. Crawford," he said without turning around. He pressed his lips against Mariah's hair before letting her slip back against the pillow. The best way to handle this, he decided, was to offer the man a handshake.

Crawford took his time in pocketing his reading glasses, folding the paper and getting to his feet to accept the gesture. "So you're the ranger."

"Seth Cantrell. I seem to have lost a couple of days, and all they would tell me was that her condition is stable. I didn't know what that meant."

Crawford lifted one eyebrow. "It means that my daughter has been through quite an ordeal. Hypothermia, exhaustion, physical and emotional abuse."

Seth looked back at Mariah, who was pushing buttons to raise the head of her bed. "It's my fault," he confessed quickly. "I never should have—"

"You're quite right. You should have sent her back

immediately. I've been in touch with the Forest Service. They tell me that if they had known—''

"We've been over this a hundred times, Dad," Mariah reminded him. "Seth wanted me to go back. I wanted to stay."

Crawford glared at Seth, who towered over him, and ignored Mariah's protest. "She hasn't confirmed this yet, but I suspect that you're the one who's responsible for my daughter's other predicament."

"If you mean the baby, you're right. It's mine."

"It's *mine*. It's inside *me*." Mariah spoke like the teacher she was, repeating patiently for those who had trouble getting the message. "And it took not one, but two of us, to put it there."

Seth gave her a conspiratorial did-it-ever look.

"It's a mistake, Mariah," Crawford insisted. "Now that you're back with me—of course, with your health seriously jeopardized by this terrible experience, not to mention your chance to make the ski team—surely you see that the only smart thing to do—''

"Are you back with him, Mariah?" Seth approached the bedside cautiously. "Is he going to make this decision for you?"

Mariah looked up, trying to send him a message with her eyes. Did he have to ask? Hadn't she already told him how she felt?

Crawford never asked. He saw only one point of view, and that was all he was capable of expressing. "Mr. Cantrell, you have no idea what it takes to build an athletic career. Mariah has always been able to rely on me for advice, for support, for protection. *Your* protection, such as it was, is no longer—''

"I think maybe my kid needs my protection."

"Dad, I'd like you to leave us alone for a while. Seth and I need to talk."

Both men looked at her. She suddenly sympathized with the creatures that were kept in classroom terrariums simply to be watched.

"All right, Mariah. I'll be as close as the phone. I always have been."

"I know that, Dad."

Seth watched the man leave, and when he turned again, he saw the tears she'd saved. They trickled over her cheeks and made him feel helpless.

Her eyes glistened, and she bunched the edge of the sheet in her hands. "He doesn't understand. Right after I got here, I was so scared I might lose the baby, and I was scared for you, and all he could say was, 'It might be the best thing.'" She waved her hand, as if to erase part of the impression she'd given. "Not about you. He…he didn't say that about you. But the baby. I needed to hear somebody else say—"

"I'm sorry." He pushed his flannel shirttail out of the way and shoved his hands into the pockets of his jeans. "I told you I wanted to help you, but I haven't gotten off to a very good start, have I?"

Mariah laid her hand on her chest. "It's my baby, Seth."

"I know. You've told me that. But I've been thinking about it, wondering—" He pulled one hand out of his pocket and gestured awkwardly, unsure where she wanted him. She patted the place beside her, and he sat down gratefully.

"Wondering what?"

"Whether it's a boy or a girl. What it's going to look like." He felt ridiculous until she offered him a tear-glittery smile and touched his thigh. He covered her hand with his. "It's bound to look like me, you know. He, she, whichever—I've got all the dominant traits."

"Lucky baby." She wiped her eyes with her free hand. "You're very handsome."

"I was worried about the baby, too," he confided. "The whole time I was following you. The baby and you, like my whole—" He stopped short of claiming that he was worried about his whole family. He didn't want to sound like such a sentimental jerk. "I didn't know whether I should ask the doctor straight out if you were still pregnant."

"They couldn't have told you that."

"I know. I've got no legal claim on your privacy, but—" She looked so small, and her face—her dear, sweet, pretty face... He shouldn't have let that happen to her. Maybe she wasn't his, but he couldn't help feeling... "I feel like I've got a right to know if he hurt you, Mariah." He touched her cheek with the backs of his fingers. "I mean, did he...?"

She closed her eyes and gave her head a quick shake. "Not that way. He kept talking about it, and the more he talked, the meaner he got. I told the police...I think he might have killed a woman. He kept saying that nobody ever found her."

"Oh, God. You must have been so scared."

"And a couple of times—" She caught her lip and bit it hard as she glanced away. She wanted to tell him, but she was afraid of what he might think. "He got kind of rough, and I thought he was going to touch me in places—" she felt the loss of his hand against her cheek, and she was afraid, but she wanted him to know "—where I don't want anyone but you to...to touch me."

"No one but me?" he asked quietly.

She flopped her hand against the bed and stared at the

blue sky through the window. "Well, I mean—" What did he think? Would it look as though she were trying to trap him if she said *love*? That first night with Seth, she hadn't objected. Not once. He wouldn't believe her if she said *love*, but maybe… "Someone I care about. Someone who cares about me." The hand that held hers tightened, and she turned to look into his eyes, where she found a hint of expectancy.

"I care about you."

"I know." But you can't say the word *love*, either. Right from the start I seemed too easy, and you're not sure…

I know I failed you, he intoned silently. Only two things I'm good for, and neither one has done you any good. But at least you should know… "I wanted to kill him myself, Mariah. When I thought of his hands on you—"

"I didn't feel it," she said quickly. "I didn't let myself feel it."

"Aw, honey, you felt it." The tears were flowing again, and he pulled her into his arms and rocked her against his chest. "It hurt you," he said, his voice raspy because it hurt him, too. "Don't ever try to tell yourself it didn't. I don't want anyone else to touch you, either."

"It wasn't like you touching me," she sobbed.

"Don't ever get the two confused."

"I couldn't confuse you with anyone."

"I know, honey. It's just that sometimes, after a nightmare like that, your mind can play tricks on you." He brushed her damp hair away from her face and tilted her chin so he could see her eyes. "If you ever get scared, you tell me, okay? I know what it's like."

"And will you tell me if you get scared?"

He glanced away from her. She'd listened to him before, but later, when he'd thought about it, he'd felt ashamed. He'd said too much. It was different for a woman. It was okay for her to be scared, but for him...maybe it was enough for her just to know that he'd been there.

"Just because we're friends," she whispered. He smiled and combed his fingers through her hair, letting himself get lost in her eyes again. Okay, so he'd told her some stuff. She hadn't looked at him like he was off his rocker. If he *had* to tell somebody something that was tearing him up, he figured maybe...just because they were friends.

She took a deep breath, trying to banish the tears. "I think it's important for our...for the baby to know when it gets a little older that at least we were friends."

He settled her back against the cranked-up bed and followed, kissing her tear-wet cheeks. "I understand that now. Friends who can touch each other—" and he did touch her gently, tenderly, through the soft cotton of the hospital gown and her nipple hardened against his palm "—in places no one else can reach."

"Oh, Seth." His touch was the only balm that could soothe her aching heart.

"Even deeper than this." He slid his hand beneath the covers and warmed her belly. "Even deeper than I can go when I make love to you."

"Only you can do that," she whispered, closing her eyes. "I can't get deep inside you."

"Oh, yes, you can, Mariah. Yes, you have."

"If you start, I won't want you to stop."

"Good," he said as he nuzzled her breast.

"You'll mess up my vital signs."

He chuckled. "We'll mess up each other's."

"Oh, that's right." Mariah looked at him as if she

were just recognizing who he was. "Should you even be out of bed?"

"No." Seth grinned. "Wanna move over?"

"I'm serious. You just got shot in the head."

He backed off with another chuckle. She was right. In another minute he would have been stroking her toward a much sweeter oblivion than the one he'd experienced in the past two days. If he got caught, Nurse Gillette would probably be trying to tie him up with tubes again.

"Do you think you'll go to Canada soon?" Mariah asked quietly.

"No." When she didn't look at him, didn't show any reaction to the news, he added, "At least, not 'til after the baby's born."

"I'm glad you're willing to help me, Seth." She started twisting the sheet again. "But I knew what I was doing. The baby's my responsibility."

"How *can* it be? You said it took two of us to put it there. Remember how we were together? How we held each other? How we—" His hand found its way to her belly again, as though at least that part of her could relate to him. "I'm part of this life, Mariah. For the first time in a long, long time, I feel as though I have something to do with life."

It was true. She had no right to deny him this. She released the crumpled sheet and put her hand on top of his. She heard him catch his breath, but she didn't look up. "I have some money," he told her. "I never had much reason to spend it, so, aside from what Carla got when we were divorced, I've just stuck it away. And I make a decent living, you know, even though it's seasonal. I could provide—"

"That isn't what I need, Seth. I can support myself and the—"

He pulled his hand away and sat up. "What do you need, then, damn it? One minute you've got your arms around my neck, and the next minute you're telling me this is *your* baby. Well, I'm the father. That's something, isn't it? Doesn't a kid need a father?"

She raised her chin and set it bravely. "If the father—"

"Look, I asked you this once, and you turned me down without giving it a second thought, but this time…" He moved closer until his thigh touched her hip, and he braced his hands on either side of her, cornering her so that they couldn't avoid each other's eyes. "This time I don't want you to say anything except that you'll think about it. Okay?"

"Okay."

"Just think about it. That's all I ask." He swallowed. "I want us to get married, Mariah. I want you to give me a chance to be a good husband and…to be a father to this baby."

Tread softly, she told herself. "Why?"

"Remember when you said you already loved this child?" She nodded. "I wanted you to tell me that you loved it because it was mine."

"Seth—"

"I know, I know. It doesn't matter. A baby is a baby, but…a long time ago, before my life got all torn up, before I even knew anything about sex, I was told that babies were born of love between two people. I stopped believing it could happen that way…until you came along." He put his hands on her shoulders and gave them a reinforcing squeeze. "The baby hasn't been born yet, and I was thinking that by that time—"

He took a deep breath to clear his head and another

for courage. "It doesn't matter how all this got started. I love you, and I love everything that's part of you."

He was like a wild thing, approaching tentatively, trying to trust. Don't rush him, she told herself before telling him, "You're part of me."

"I know." It was a start, and he wanted to make something of it. It was more than he'd ever had before. "That's what I was thinking. I was thinking, if she can love this child of mine, maybe she can love me, too."

"I do love you, Seth, and it isn't because I'm carrying your child."

He looked at her curiously, as if he didn't think he'd heard her right. She wouldn't lie. She'd been up-front with him all along about not needing him for anything.

"I said I love you, Seth. If I hadn't been pregnant, I might never have seen you again, but I was, and I did, and that's when…" She smiled and laid her hand on his cheek. "*That's* when all this got started."

"I want the baby," he told her. He seemed dazed.

"I do, too."

"And I want to marry you."

"You asked me to think about it." Her smile widened. "Which is what I intend to do."

"For how long? When can I kiss the bride?"

"Don't count your—"

Her warning was cut short by a long, hard, joy-filled kiss from the father of her unborn, *to be* born, child. Seth had stopped counting chickens long ago. He counted bears. He counted wolves where there weren't any, and he'd once counted his chances with a woman like Mariah as slim to nonexistent.

Right now, he counted himself a very lucky man.

Epilogue

The dampness of the spring earth seeped through the knees of Mariah's jeans. She gripped the wrought-iron porch railing in her left hand and stretched to reach behind a spindly rose bush with her garden fork. She'd come to terms with the fact that anything she did these days was done awkwardly around a barrel of a belly, and the view of her backside certainly added nothing to the front yard's curb appeal. The previous tenants had apparently let the yard fend for itself, but she was determined to have flowers. Despite the twinge in her back, she knew that if she was going to get the beds cleaned out, she had to get it done today.

A long, low wolf whistle brought her head around. Seth laughed as he hitched his thumb in his hip pocket and stepped closer. She'd braced the heels of her hands in the rich black loam, and she reminded him of a bear cub looking for its tail.

"You're gonna cause a traffic jam on Kalispell's quietest street, Mrs. Cantrell.''

"Only if Mr. Cantrell backs the Blazer out into the street and kills the engine.'' Mariah managed a roly-poly reversal, plopping her bottom in the dirt. She brushed her hands together briskly, succeeding only in making them blacker, and smiled up at him. He'd been pruning trees in the backyard, and she'd heard him humming and singing snatches of tunes now and then. If she'd paid attention to the sudden quiet, he wouldn't have caught her by surprise.

He stood on the grassy slope, his jeans and black T-shirt giving him the look of a young tough, his hair damp from sweat. She suspected that the hand behind his back held another of his wonderful little surprises. It might be a glass of milk or an earthworm he'd dug up in the backyard. She'd learned to be ready for anything. "When you're as fat as I am, you don't stop traffic unless you're jaywalking,'' she told him.

"You're pregnant, not fat, and I don't want to catch you stretching like that anymore. You remember what Mom said about that.''

"That I shouldn't hang clothes on the line or do any reaching because the cord might get wrapped around the baby's neck,'' Mariah recited from memory.

She flexed her shoulders back and forth as she pressed her fingers into the small of her back. She and Seth had spent Christmas on his parents' South Dakota farm just after they were married, and his mother had compiled a list of dos and don'ts for the expectant mother. Her presence and her pregnancy had seemed to ease some of the strain between the senior Cantrells and their estranged son. No mention was made of his long absence. Like his wartime experiences and his stay in the VA hospital, the

Cantrells didn't discuss what they couldn't accept or understand. With Mariah's help, Seth had made his peace with that fact.

For their part, Seth and Mariah dealt openly with remembered terror, and they were learning that the haunting memories faded when they held each other in the dark. Once all the testimony had been given and the reports had been filed, putting Mariah's abduction behind them became easier. Seth had begun to forgive himself for leaving her alone in the cabin. The law had been lenient with Gordie Morton, who had told investigators everything they'd wanted to know about his father. In the three years since he had been living in the isolated regions of the Rockies with his son, Oliver Morton, alias Ray McKenzie, had murdered one woman, harassed others and done a lot of poaching. Gordie's information had led to the discovery of the victim's remains.

"No point in taking any chances." Seth squatted on the heels of his tennis shoes in the greening thatch of grass he'd raked earlier. He looked into his wife's eyes, green as spring shoots, and she looked back at him. Feminine laughter bubbled first, then the masculine echo. Since that night at Telly's, Mariah had become an expert at taking chances. Chance had posed its threats, but chance had also brought them together. In honor of life's ironies and the warm spring weather and the way his wife's hair captured the sunbeams, Seth produced a bunch of purple blossoms from behind his back.

"Irises!" Mariah held out her hands for the bouquet. "Where did you find them?"

"Under a pile of leaves in the backyard. And I've pruned the birches and picked up all the pinecones and raked and—" If she was listening, he wouldn't have known it. The flowers had claimed her attention. The delicate petals complemented her pink cheeks and rosy mouth. "Don't move, honey. I'll be right back."

Mariah groaned. Of late Seth had developed a penchant for taking pictures of her, and she had never felt less photogenic. Sure enough, he was back in a flash with the damn camera.

"Seth, I look like I'm wearing a tablecloth under Aunt Bertha's sweater, and my knees are dirty, and..."

It was no use. The camera clicked and whirred. She hoped the flowers minimized the big round belly and the wet brown circles on her knees.

"Lift your face toward the sun."

She closed her eyes and followed instructions. "Why do you do this?" she purred, deeply pleased that he did.

"Because I'm a nature photographer, and you're the image of Mother Nature." She treated him to a throaty laugh. "And guess what came in the mail today?"

"What?"

"A letter from *Great Outdoors* magazine. They want to use some of my stuff in a book they're publishing."

Mariah's eyes flew open, and her face radiated the sunlight it had just absorbed. "Seth, that's wonderful!"

"Of course, I still plan to work for the Forest Service in the summer."

"Which is fine, because you'll be doing a lot of babysitting while I'm teaching." She held the purple blooms to her nose and flashed smiling eyes above them. "Our careers dovetail nicely, don't they?"

"*We* dovetail nicely."

"Dad brought over a gift for the baby today," she told him. "A child carrier. He says we'll need it when we go hiking, and that I should keep in shape just in case."

Still squatting on his heels, he braced his forearms over his thighs and laced his fingers together loosely. "Whenever you wanna strap on a pair of skis, you just let me know. I'll be right there—''

"I thought you didn't—"

"At the lodge, waiting for you." Smiling warmly, he planted one knee in the grass and leaned over to spread his hand over her hard, round belly. "Your dad thinks he might make a skier out of his grand—hey!" His face always got soft with wonder when he felt the life within his wife's womb. "This kid's on the move."

Mariah sat up straight and worked her fingers against her lower back again. "He can move out any time now."

"Your back hurts, huh? Come here." She offered no resistance as he sat on the grass and drew her to sit between his legs. "Lean back and let me do that for you."

"We're sitting right out on the front lawn," she reminded him as she dropped her head back against his shoulder. His hands felt so much better on her back than her own did.

"So what? We're dressed." Then he lowered his voice near her ear. "I'm only imagining we're not."

"You're fantasizing about giving a back rub to a naked hippo?"

"Your stomach is beautiful, just like the rest of you, but I have a feeling it's getting kind of heavy for you." In sympathy, he kissed the corner of her forehead. "I wish I could carry it for you when you get tired like this."

"The baby carrier from Dad will fit you nicely."

Seth responded with a cheeky cluck. "There's only one thing that came from *Dad* that fits me nicely."

"Seth…"

She drawled his name, and he laughed. "You sound more like a wife all the time."

"Well, he *did* apologize—sort of." The back pain had

begun to radiate around her sides, and she reached back and moved his hands. "Do this," she murmured, showing him where to stroke.

"I don't think you should have been digging around in the dirt here—especially after getting up at five o'clock this morning to clean the cupboards. They didn't even need cleaning, honey. We just moved in, and we did all that kind of stuff."

"I wanted to make sure."

"Well, they're sure clean now, and I'm beat." Seth nuzzled Mariah's hair, while beneath her cardigan he caressed her bulging sides in slow circles. "Didn't the doctor say it could start in your back?"

"Mmm-hmm."

He was quiet for a moment. "So, how long has it been?"

"Maybe an hour. I think this is the real thing."

"What does it feel like?"

"Like it could be the start of something big."

She giggled, but he wasn't laughing. "Wanna go inside?"

"Not yet. I want to sit here with you and enjoy the sun for just a few more minutes. Then I want to take a bath and shave my legs."

His hands stilled. "Shave your legs!"

"Please don't stop."

Obediently he resumed the massage. "Does this help?"

"It helps me feel a little less scared."

Mariah had a right to be scared, but why was his heart thumping a mile a minute all of a sudden? Mother Nature didn't require much of him. He was like the seed drill his dad had on the farm. Once his part was done, Mariah could have handled the rest without complicating his reclusive existence. But she'd climbed his mountain, and he felt blessed.

"For whatever it's worth, I'm with you all the way, honey."

She covered his hands with hers and held them tight against her. "It's worth everything."

* * * * *

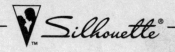

SPECIAL EDITION™

Emotional, compelling stories that capture the intensity of living, loving and creating a family in today's world.

Desire

Modern, passionate reads that are powerful and provocative.

nocturne

Dramatic and sensual tales of paranormal romance.

Romantic SUSPENSE

Romances that are sparked by danger and fueled by passion.

Silhouette®

SPECIAL EDITION™

Emotional, compelling stories that capture the intensity of living, loving and creating a family in today's world.

Special Edition features bestselling authors such as Susan Mallery, Sherryl Woods, Christine Rimmer, Joan Elliott Pickart— and many more!

For a romantic, complex and emotional read, choose Silhouette Special Edition.

Silhouette®

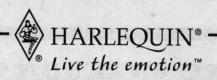

HARLEQUIN®

Live the emotion™

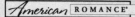

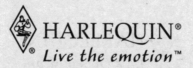

HARLEQUIN®
INTRIGUE®

BREATHTAKING ROMANTIC SUSPENSE

Shared dangers and passions lead to electrifying romance and heart-stopping suspense!

Every month, you'll meet six new heroes who are guaranteed to make your spine tingle and your pulse pound. With them you'll enter into the exciting world of Harlequin Intrigue— where your life is on the line and so is your heart!

THAT'S INTRIGUE— ROMANTIC SUSPENSE AT ITS BEST!

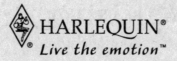

HARLEQUIN®
Live the emotion™

HARLEQUIN®

Super Romance®

...there's more to the story!

Superromance.
A *big* satisfying read about unforgettable characters. Each month we offer *six* very different stories that range from family drama to adventure and mystery, from highly emotional stories to romantic comedies—and much more! Stories about people you'll believe in and care about. Stories too compelling to put down....

Our authors are among today's *best* romance writers. You'll find familiar names and talented newcomers. Many of them are award winners—and you'll see why!

If you want the biggest and best in romance fiction, you'll get it from Superromance!

Exciting, Emotional, Unexpected...

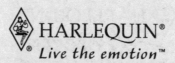

HARLEQUIN®
Live the emotion™

HARLEQUIN®
Presents~

The world's bestselling romance series...
The series that brings you your favorite authors,
month after month:

Helen Bianchin...Emma Darcy
Lynne Graham...Penny Jordan
Miranda Lee...Sandra Marton
Anne Mather...Carole Mortimer
Susan Napier...Michelle Reid

and many more uniquely talented authors!

Wealthy, powerful, gorgeous men...
Women who have feelings just like your own...
The stories you love, set in exotic, glamorous locations...

HARLEQUIN®
Presents~
Seduction and Passion Guaranteed!

www.eHarlequin.com

HPDIR104